CONTENTS

CONTENTS

Mirror Mirror, Who's the Killer?

→

Wyld Enchantment Woods
Cozy Mystery

Kura Jane Carpenter

WUP
Wicked Unicorn Press

Published by **Wicked Unicorn Press**

National Library of New Zealand Cataloguing-in-Publication Data
Mirror mirror, who's the killer? / Kura Jane Carpenter
ebook ISBN 978-1-99-117720-9
softcover ISBN 978-1-99-117721-6

Map of Ella's Home

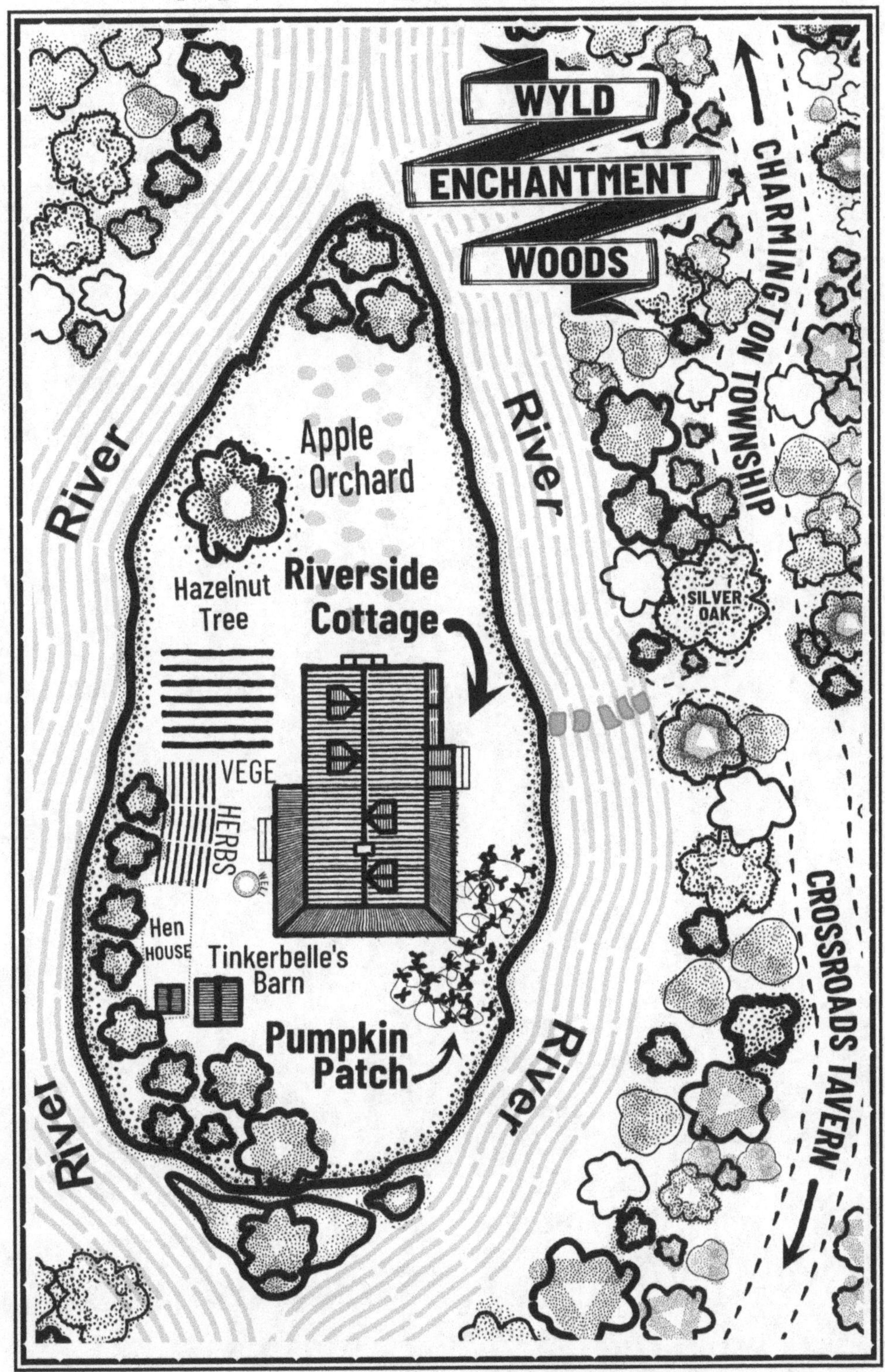

Chapter 1

Market Day

"The queen broke her magic mirror?"

"Uh huh, cracked the glass in two." The tiny lady with the pink bouffant hairdo standing in front of Ella's soup stall mimed a hand flick. "I was just going in to do her hair and–smack! Hurled it against the wall."

"But whatever for, Goldi? It's worth—"

"A king's ransom, I know, I know."

Ella mulled over this information as she ladled a scoop of her gelatinous pumpkin soup from the cauldron to splat into the wooden bowl Goldilocks presented. Around the pair the Charmington Saturday morning market was a bustling hive of goods, trade and gossip, come first thing or last thing, summer or winter. Well, winter. It was always winter in Wyld kingdom now, thanks to you-know-who.

Ella drew her black woollen cloak tight across her thin chest to ward off the chill mountain air. "And do you know what the mirror said that upset our dear, beloved queen?" she asked, shaking the last stubborn drops of soup free from the brass ladle.

"If you're asking if it was another dreadful prophecy, I didn't hear the mirror say anything and I didn't hang around. You know what Sibylla's like when she throws a tantrum." Goldilocks suppressed a grimace and then bobbed a dainty curtsey. "Thanks for the soup. It looks, er, yum. How do you always get it so thick? Anyways, I'd best be off, here's my donation for the hospital." She popped two silver coins into the little bucket beside the soup cauldron on which the hand-painted sign once read *Cinderella Charity Animal Sanctuary* but now read *ella Charity Animal*.

"Aren't you going to have a spoonful before you go?" Ella voiced, as her cat Tilly, who had been curled up tight on the hessian sack of kindling, cracked her green eyes up at her mistress.

"Er, well, it's just you haven't lit the fire under the cauldron today...so the soup is cold." Goldilocks blinked. "Was there a...special...reason for that?"

"Oh no, I just couldn't get the tinder lit. It got a bit damp," Ella apologised. From the curled bundle of snow-white fluff, Tilly yawned, and then nuzzled deeper into the hessian sack as if to say she didn't see the need for a fire anyway.

"Why didn't you ask anyone for help?" The little craftswoman cast a covert glance at the northern wall of the market square, on which was painted in thick black letters across the grey stone blocks: *Magic is forbidden.*

Standing under the painted warning, the girl who worked at the Crossroads tavern, Robinne, was slouched against the stone wall. In front of the lass, a selection of tall brown bottles had been set out on an upturned barrel. Robinne wore her customary scarlet woollen cloak, the hood so low over her forehead that her eyes weren't visible.

Was she asleep? Typical youth, always caught up in the moment and never thinking about tomorrow. Probably spent all night spouting politics at the tavern... Not that it was any of her business, Ella reminded herself.

Goldilocks sneezed and the tinder at the base of the tripod burst into flame. "I guess it just needed more time to ignite."

"Magic preserve me, 'tis a miracle," Ella muttered drolly and grabbed pinecones from the sack Tilly nested upon. "Does it make that much of a difference, served hot...?"

"Of course not! And now I have the perfect excuse–reason, for saving this for later, for lunch today," blustered the small lady while stooping to tickle Tilly under the chin, almost as if she wanted to avoid Ella's eye.

"I do love to see how much you enjoy it," Ella insisted suspiciously. Surely Goldi liked the soup? Everyone always told her how much nicer it was since she removed the skins, even Arthur and he owned a cafe now and knew a thing or two about cooking. Ella admitted she'd had a shaky start, having never cooked for herself when she lived at the castle but... "Oh, it's still terrible, isn't it? I tell myself surely it's improved, but who am I fooling? I should go back to candy apples. At least they were tasty even though they rot your teeth..."

"Nonsense, it's fine, I just forgot my spoon!" Goldilocks slapped her forehead. "Goodness, speaking of forgetful, I must be off, I've still got to do Sibylla's hair before the big announcement!" The little lady turned and disappeared into the crowd, only her immaculate bouffant visible as she wove through the Charmington townsfolk.

Ella tapped her toe and glanced up at the queen's balcony, then back at the faded sign on her donations bucket. The last time the family magic mirror had spoken a prophecy their sister Cinderella had died and Ella's life fell apart.

Wishing not for the first time she still had her wand and her powers; Ella pushed the regret deep down. Feeling sorry for herself wasn't going to fill the charity bucket! There were more injured animals out there that needed her help, just like Tilly had once. Although in truth, hadn't Tilly saved her? Saved her from facing another night of endless winter all alone in her cottage deep in Wyld Enchantment Woods.

"Lawks, I've dust in my eye," Ella muttered out of habit while blinking away the sudden, irksome sting of regret. Hold your head high and carry on, that was her motto.

Turning her eye wipe into a casual stretch, Ella looked around the marketplace. She had planned on buying a loaf of salt-crust sourdough for her and Tilly's dinner. A slice of buttery toast beside the fire tonight would chase away her foolish melancholy, but there was no sign of the baker's stall. "Robinne, dear," Ella called loudly to the sleeping teenager, "have you seen your aunt Ginny today? I'm out of bread."

"Has it occurred to you that there might be more important things going on than sourdough?" Robinne grumbled, pushing the hood from her eyes when at that moment across the way the clip-clop of a pony's hooves, echoing through the portcullis archway, preceded Baker Bron's cart rolling into view.

"Never mind, dear, there they are," Ella replied with false cheer, "you can go back to your rebellious act of napping."

But only Baker Bron crossed the wooden bridge into the market square and without a nod or other greeting to any of the other stall holders, jumped down from his cart to set up his trestle table.

Odd, usually Ginny manned the couple's stall at the weekly market.

Ella wandered over and helped the ginger-haired baker spread a red and white checked cloth across the rough-hewn wooden tabletop. From the back of the cart, Baker Bron unpacked willow baskets of baked goods. Ella eyed the overly browned loaves and gingerbread men with burnt toes. Ginny loved to decorate the little biscuits, giving each one its own personality. She would never sell un-iced biscuits let alone burnt ones. "Where's your wife, Ginny?"

"Sick," Bron muttered, not meeting her eye. He had bags under his eyes and his clothes were wrinkled and covered in more flour than usual.

Mind your own business, old woman, Ella scolded herself and led Bron's fat pony to be hitched beside her own donkey Tinkerbelle. She clasped the water-pump handle and refreshed the trough for the pair.

Above the castle courtyard, the ornate lead-glass door to the queen's balcony suddenly opened, "Absurdity!" rang out Sibylla's voice, "The mirror lies! I am queen!" and then the door banged shut.

"Our queen is having a bad day," Ella said, scratching Tinkerbelle between her soft, grey ears.

"She's not *my* queen," Robinne muttered, crossing her arms, her breathing fanning out in indignation on this frosty morning.

Nor mine, Ella thought, but aloud said, "And how goes the revolution?" before threading her way through the market goers to her side of the marketplace. Magic preserve, the lass should learn to hold her tongue. Keep her head down and stay out of trouble.

"Only cowards stay silent." Robinne pushed off from the wall and went to trade a bottle of dark bitter brew with Baker Bron for a suspiciously solid-looking roll and burnt gingerbread man.

"Cowards get fewer people hanged," Ella muttered to herself as she thought over the fragment she'd heard Sibylla spout.

Whatever could the mirror have said to upset her sister? Sibylla *was* queen, that was indisputable. But being 'queen' didn't equate to a life free from irritation. Ella had discovered that life was full of unwelcome nonsense. People you loved died. People you loved didn't love you back. Best to shut everyone out, then you had no one but yourself to blame. Yes, indeed. That was the truth.

"Are you helping me draw in customers today?" Ella addressed Tilly. From the curled bundle of snow-white fluff, Tilly opened one green eye, yawned and then nuzzled deeper into the hessian sack. "People don't want to pat an old lady," Ella told her unhelpful cat. "They know I bite."

Ella inspected the orange mush in her cook-pot as heavy boots echoed across the bridge and two of Queen Sibylla's henchmen entered the courtyard. Axel Luther, Sibylla's Head Henchman, was shaking his finger at a fresh-faced recruit.

"Do I get to ring the bell?" the younger blond man asked, eyes fixed on the heavy brass handbell which Axel lugged over one shoulder.

Magic preserve! Ella experienced a jolt of *déjà vu*. The young blond henchman bore a striking resemblance to Arthur, a monarch in the neighbouring kingdom of Avalon. Was this *doppelgänger* a young prince pretending to be a commoner?

Ella huffed. What a lousy idea. Tricking innocent people. Come to think of it, that had been Arthur's sense of humour, the odious man!

"No way." Axel waved off the plea. "Bell ringing is the captain's duty. Watch and learn, junior."

The young blond recruit nodded studiously as Axel plonked the bell down and began ripping old wanted posters from the official noticeboard.

Despite the current lesson in administrative paperwork, the recruit's attention wandered and was caught by the slim form of Robinne basking in the watery sun. Her hair spilt in luxurious dark curls as she pushed back her red hood to reveal an attractive heart-shaped face.

"Good day." The young man approached Robinne, eyeing her collection of brews. "Elderflower, Thistle, Black currant..." he read the labels aloud. "They sound *enchanting*."

Robinne bit the head off her gingerbread man. "Don't sell to *lackeys*."

The young henchman held up his rather large hands, palms outwards. "Pardon my presumption." He stepped back and turned away, not wearing a look of dejection, as Ella had expected, but a smile.

Odd, very odd. "You're wasting your time with that one," Ella said as the young henchman crossed the cobbles and loomed over her cauldron now bubbling thickly with soft, pumpkin plops.

His smile only deepened as if pleased to accept a challenge. "Master Spicer says, a friend hard won is twice as loyal."

Ella stared up at the boy. He certainly had the build for henching, six-foot going on seven if he was an inch!

"What a beautiful cat," the lad crouched down and peered curiously at Tilly.

"You can pet her if you're gentle," Ella offered.

The lad looked abashed and stood up to loom over her again. "Wish I could, I wanted to apprentice to a vet, but I'm allergic to cats..."

"Um…" Ella found herself saying, "has anybody ever said you look like the king?"

The lad patted his downy cheeks. "That's partly why Master Spicer made me grow this beard and take a summer job out of the city… He said, 'Tom, from the right angle you resemble Prince John a bit and if someone notices–well, you don't want to end up like Davis.'"

"Davis?" Ella blinked.

"A boy…who sort of vanished. I mean, they found most of him. Eventually." The young henchman shuddered. "Anyway, it's silly, sure every orphan wants to secretly be the long-lost son of someone special, but Prince John is barely thirty and I'm twenty-three! So what if we have the same nose?"

Ella dredged her memories for Prince John, she recalled a sharp-eyed child she'd met about twenty-five years ago at some banquet. "I meant King Arthur, from Avalon, not John from Sherwood," Ella corrected.

"King Arthur!" Tom laughed. "He died decades ago! Gosh, you must be really, *really* old."

"How rude!" Ella muttered under her breath. Old, was she? Well, she'd been telling herself all morning to mind her own business and it was high time she took her own advice! From here on in the lad could look after himself!

Licking his lips, the lad pulled a horn spoon from his pocket. "Pumpkin?"

His question jolted Ella and reminded her purpose for being there.

When had she last stirred…? She dug the ladle deep into the soup, sluggishly scraping the bottom, turning over black burnt bits and seeds.

"Looks…" He swallowed hesitantly but patted the coin pouch belted to his hip. "A serving if I may?"

"Oh…" Ella shrugged. Helpless. "My regulars bring their own bowls, see." She squinted up at him in the frosty air. Lawks, he was a biggun.

The lad's pleasant face clouded. Then brightening, he rushed over to Baker Bron who spluttered something, immediately handed over a loaf of bread and then stood back gaping at the formidable presence and then blinked at the two coppers in his hand when the queen's newest henchman actually paid him.

Poking a hollow into the tough bread, the young man returned to Ella's stall and announced, "Bowl!"

"Uh-huh." Ella took the offered bread and scooped a large helping within. "And you are?"

He bowed low. "Forgive my manners. Tom April at your service."

April? Named after a month, definitely an orphan then... A polite henchman at my service? Magic preserve, what an odd day.

Ella glanced over at Baker Bron, still clearly startled at being paid. Axel never paid. Just leered at Ginny and licked the icing off the biscuits. She handed the bread and thick orange contents over.

Tom held out his palm in return, a selection of coins presented. "What's the usual donation?"

Ella shook her head. "First bowl is on me... Have you been a henchman long, Tom?"

Tom laughed. "Guardsman, we prefer *guardsman*."

Potato, pot*arto*, Ella thought with an internal shrug.

"And just a few weeks. I love all the snow here. It's like Christmas every day." He took a large spoonful of pumpkin and shovelled it into his mouth. His eyes went wide. He blinked. Eventually, he pushed the mush from one side of his mouth to the other.

Maybe it was too hot? Ella folded her thin arms. "To your liking, Tom April-at-my-service?"

Tom chewed. Cracking was audible. He swallowed. "Crunchier than it looks."

The creak of door hinges above made Ella look up at the castle.

Queen Sibylla strutted out onto the balcony. Dressed in gold and purple, her sumptuous silk skirts accentuated her tiny waist and curvy figure. With sharp features, full red lips and pale skin she was striking. Her long dark chestnut hair was unbound, giving her an appearance of youthfulness, as if no more than thirty.

Ella tucked a strand of greying hair that had escaped from her tight bun. Appearances were deceptive. They were the same age. *Exactly* the same age, given that they were twins. Though as far as most of the world knew, they were strangers.

Their eyes met. Sibylla's scarlet lips curled back to reveal perfect teeth. Scowling wasn't unexpected, but she usually wore a smirk when lording her good fortune over Ella.

"Well?" Sibylla glared down on her milling subjects.

Baker Bron swiftly removed his cap. "Three cheers for the queen!"

"Hip-*rah*! Hip-*rah*! Hip-*rah*!" Tom April joined in enthusiastically with the crowd gathering under the balcony.

Ella twirled a finger in the air. "Huzzah. Much cheering."

"Get on with it!" Sibylla commanded; her voice icy as the snow-covered ridgeline that surrounded her mountaintop castle.

Axel cleared his throat. "Right, listen up, Charmington rabble." He stood back from the noticeboard and gave the bell a half-hearted shake. *Clang*.

"Hear-ye, hear-ye, by decree of Queen Sibylla, *lawful* and *rightful* ruler of Wyld kingdom, a week tomorrow there shall be a grand archery competition!" Axel paused to point a finger at Bron, who clutched his chest as if stabbed, and then Robinne, whose lip-curling expression mimicked the queen's look of disgust, before he carried on, "A prize of one thousand gold coins awaits the winner!"

Ella gasped. Robinne stood upright. Bron blinked.

Tom April gave his superior the thumbs up while mouthing, "Great speech, boss!"

That was a lot of money – a lot of a lot! One hundred gold coins was more than a year's wages. But to give away one thousand! Ella shared a look with Robinne who for once dropped her tough act and looked as stunned as Bron. What was Sibylla up to?

Axel shut one eye, as if thinking. "Oh yes... ahem, all magic is forbidden!" He puffed out his chest. "Anyone caught performing, selling, aiding or abetting dark magics shall be dealt with most harshly." He flourished a gloved hand to the darkest recesses of the square where dilapidated gallows lurked like a toad at a swan convention.

Sibylla made a noise of disgust and slammed the balcony door shut behind her. Beneath Ella's cauldron the flames suddenly puffed out in a crack of roiling black smoke. Beside her, Tom April flinched. One of his large feet caught the tripod stand and the whole contraption tipped over with a bang.

"Oops," said Axel, with a smirk.

Ella held her tongue as the thick orange slop steamed and oozed over the cobbles.

Tom grabbed the ladle and tried scooping the soup back into the cauldron. "I'm so sorry!"

Ella sighed and patted his broad shoulders. "There, there, lad, let it be. It could be worse." Her eyes unbidden sought the gallows. "After all, no one died."

Chapter 2

Be careful what you wish for

Tink Tink Tink

Ella woke from dozing in her rocking chair. Embers glowed in the hearth, illuminating the timbers of her snug parlour. Above the rough-hewn oak mantel, the string of crystal fairy lights blinked and *tinked* their soft yet urgent crystalline chimes of warning.

Tink Tink Tink

Ella sat up. Fully awake. Someone must have entered her garden.

Tilly was already aware. Ready for action, the cat's claws scratched at the foot of the door.

Ella eased her stiff bones out of the chair and picked up the fire poker. She went to a window and peered through the rippled glass, out to the pumpkin patch beyond her porch. In the moonlit yard, a large shadowy figure tripped and stumbled as the vines shifted and stretched like snakes.

"Well now, it's been a long time since we've had a thief for tea," Ella told her cat. "This could be fun."

She hobbled down the hall to the front door and lifted the latch. Tilly zoomed past, a ball of indignant white fur, near invisible across the freshly fallen snow. Drawing her knitted shawl close over her threadbare dressing gown, Ella called out as she limped to the porch edge. "Who's there, dearie?"

"Argh!" the figure started, twisted about. A panicked youthful face glanced over. "Something bit me!"

Ella let out her breath. "Tom April?"

"I could've sworn there was a path." The lad lifted one foot, ankle snagged with vines. "I saw the light from your cottage, thought it was the tavern—urgh!" With that, he fell over heavily and the vines continued to wind about his legs. "Hey, quit that! Help!"

Tilly pranced around, lithe of foot, running back and forth between the edge of the pumpkin patch and the porch steps.

"Hold on, I'm coming." Ella gripped the handrail. "Play dead, that'll confuse them."

"Them?" He thrashed about in the snowy moonlit garden as the vines writhed.

"The pumpkins, they're carnivorous." Using the poker as a walking stick, Ella shuffled over to the stricken form trussed up in her vegetable garden.

Tilly pounced onto Tom's chest and hissed in his face.

"Listen to Tilly and lie still," Ella instructed as the stealthy vines kept on wrapping about him. "The more you wriggle the more you encourage them."

"I'm allergic to cats." Tom wiggled to shoo her but gave up as Tilly wasn't going anywhere and settled in to groom herself on his chest. "I love them but I break out in big hives and itch like crazy."

Ella glanced upwards as the sky darkened, drifting clouds obscuring the full moon. A shooting star flashed across the inky night.

"I *wish* I could trade lives with you." Tom sighed at her feet. "Then I could pet cats."

No! Ella scrunched her eyes tight shut. Held her breath.

A shooting star!

A wish!

She dropped the poker. Patted her thin chest. *Still me...?*

Ella let out a long breath.

Still me! Silly old woman...

She bent to pick up the poker and then tapped the vines. "Release him. You've had your fun."

The vines shuddered, rippled, then unfurled, grudgingly releasing their prey.

"See Tom, thy day is getting better." She scooped up Tilly as Tom flailed, kicking and flapping arms everywhere. "Steady, lad!" Ella clutched Tilly's warmth to her, the cat rigid in her grasp. "Be careful of my precious cat!"

Tom rolled over, shrugged off the last of the receding plants, and pushed up on all fours. He lurched as he got to his feet. Wild-eyed he tottered at full height and then sprinted out of the garden towards the frozen stream at the edge of the surrounding forest.

"The Crossroads tavern is that way, over yonder!" She pointed to a gap in the trees, but Tom wasn't listening.

He bound, lithe of foot, steppingstone to steppingstone, across the iced-over river and darted into the dark pines.

"How's that for manners?" Ella muttered, stroking Tilly. The small cat wriggled in her arms. "Tilly?"

"W...w...w..." Tilly panted and held her paws in front of her whiskers. Green eyes blinked wide. "Witch!" the cat rasped. "Witch! What have you done to meeee?"

CHAPTER 3

OOPS

ELLA COCKED HER HEAD. "Tom? Is that you? Are you in there?" She put the squirming cat down.

"What's going on?" The cat—Tom—Tomcat patted his new body. "I'm covered in fur!"

Magic preserve me. Ella sighed and drawing her shawl close said, "Come wait inside, I'm sure Tilly will be back with your body soon."

"But...but...the midnight coach leaves from the tavern." Tomcat pointed to the fir trees at the river's edge. "I have to catch it. I have urgent and important business for the queen!"

"Urgent and important, well then." Ella hesitated. The coach was monthly. Did she really want to spend a whole month stuck with one of Sibylla's henchmen? "Let me swap my slippers for boots..."

Once inside the warmth of her cottage, Ella toed off her sheepskin slippers and laced on her stout walking boots. Her favourite black woollen cloak she put on over top of her dressing gown for extra padding, tucked a scarf about her throat, and then glanced at the cluckoo clock ticking softly above the mantelpiece. The brass hands read 11.25 pm.

Still time if they hurried.

Scooping up her proper walking stick from beside the front door she headed back out into the garden.

"Quickly, quickly, he's getting away!" Tomcat danced from one foot to the other.

He's...?

Tilly was female. Ella shook her head. Not that it mattered. This would all be sorted shortly and she wouldn't be having *that* awkward conversation with Tom.

Tomcat was shivering. A forlorn, confused, little bundle of fluff on the icy earth. Unthinkingly Ella unwrapped her scarf and swept the small cat up in it, but Tomcat hissed, squirmed from Ella's grasp and dropped to the snowy ground.

"Stay back, Witch!"

Ella rolled her eyes. "I am not a witch."

"Yes, you are!" Green eyes stared up accusingly. "See! You turned me into a cat! I'm going to tell everyone!"

Leaning over, in order to glower better, Ella replied, "*I* didn't turn you into a cat, Tom April—*you* were the one making wishes under shooting stars while standing in a magical pumpkin patch."

Tomcat huffed and crossed his paws across his chest. "Wait till the queen finds out. Magic is forbidden!"

"Good point." Ella pivoted about.

"Hey! Where're you going?"

"Back inside." Ella snapped over her shoulder as she shuffled towards her porch and its welcoming light spilling from the windows. "It's cold and dark and you are very rude!"

Tomcat caught up to her—running on his two hind legs—and tugged the back of her skirts. "But I need your help."

Resting heavily on the walking stick, Ella turned and said, "Maybe you should try apologising?"

"I am sorry! I'm sorry I ever came here! I'm sorry you are mean and make the worst soup I have ever tasted!" Tomcat clamped a paw to his whiskers. "Oops—I didn't mean to say that part out loud."

Ella regarded Tomcat standing on two legs. Lawks that looked unnatural! "Stop walking upright like a person. You're..." What was it the youngsters said? "...freaking me out."

Tomcat rubbed his fluffy white belly. "But the ground is cold on my tummy."

Ella threw her head back and laughed. She laughed and laughed. Her laughter spilt out, fat clouds of chuckles rolling onto the frosted night air.

When was the last time she'd laughed?

Gathering her wits, she tightened the ties of her cloak and clasped the walking stick firmly.

She contemplated bringing a lantern, but the moon had reappeared, illuminating the snow-shrouded firs quite adequately. Besides, if Tilly was feeling playful a lantern would give them away and make catching her all the harder.

"Right, Tom April, let's go find your body."

Walking slower than was strictly necessary, Ella shuffled across the iced-over river that surrounded her little island on which Riverside Cottage was built.

It wasn't that she missed having people to talk to, of course not, it was just why shouldn't Tilly enjoy a few more minutes as a very tall human? That would be a treat. This misadventure was entirely Tom's fault anyhow, if he wanted to go making wishes on stars well then, let him live and learn that there were consequences.

"How goes the guardsman life, Tom April?" Ella asked conversationally as she peered at the fresh snow on the riverbank and deciphered cat paw prints. "This way, follow me."

"It started well, I met so many great people...but... Admittedly, this morning was the worst," came the lament from Tomcat, walking on his hind legs he gripped Ella's skirt for balance as they trekked under the trees.

"Really? Worse than being eaten by carnivorous pumpkins or being turned into a cat?" Ella paused to get her bearings. The main path was ahead, between the giant silver oak and the cluster of pines.

His cat ears dipped. "Do you know what I did today?"

"What?" Ella paused, listening. Was that rustling ahead? "I think we're close..." She glanced down at Tom, he looked forlorn.

"I evicted a family from the cuckoo shop."

Ah. So the lad had had a proper dose of henching and it wasn't to his taste. It wasn't all bellringing and chatting up pretty girls. Perhaps there was hope for him.

"*Cluck*-oo," Ella corrected, not unkindly, carrying on walking. Yes! Something was happening up ahead. She could see someone. "Black Forest has cuckoos, in Wyld Woods we make cluckoos with roosters. They crow, don't hoot."

He wasn't listening. Caught up in his memory. "I felt terrible! But if I didn't do it Axel said I'd be fired! Then how could I send money to Master Spicer and the orphans? I can't afford another failed job! Can things get any worse?"

Ella stopped short. On the path ahead crouched Baker Bron, a longbow in one hand, and at his feet, Tom April's human body. Lying motionless on the snow. An arrow shaft protruded from Tom's chest.

Chapter 4

Tom's Day Gets Worse

Wyld Enchantment Woods.

"Magic preserve!" Ella dropped her walking stick in surprise. At her feet, Tomcat gagged and collapsed. "Bron, what have you done?"

The baker stood, face aghast. "It's not what it looks like! I didn't do this!" Bron clutched his hand to his breastbone and then gestured imploringly at the stricken form of Tom, on his back, still as the grave, an arrow shaft jutting like an accusation. "Good mother Ella, you must believe me! I saw a cloaked figure standing over him—searching him," Bron babbled. "I thought they were robbing him. I shouted and they ran." He pointed down. Clear footprints were visible in the snow. "See look, they went that way into the trees."

Ella observed the fresh tracks. One set indeed going off in the direction Bron indicated. And another set along the main track heading to the tavern. So possibly two or three others had encountered or crossed paths with young Tom/Tilly.

Ella picked up the now whimpering Tomcat and thrust him into Bron's arms. "Hold my cat."

"What?"

"Just do it, he's going into shock, keep him warm." Using the walking stick for support she lowered herself to the ground. Freeing one glove with her teeth, she placed a bare hand on the skin of Tom's exposed throat.

Warm... But still alive?

She regarded the black arrow piercing the folds of his cloak. How deep had it gone? There didn't seem to be a lot of blood, but it was too dark to be sure. "Baker, have you a hand mirror? I need to check if he's breathing."

"Why would *I* have a mirror?" Bron retorted, awkwardly clutching both Tomcat and the longbow.

"Why are you aimlessly wandering Wyld Enchantment Woods?" Ella asked over her shoulder. "When you should be tucked-up warm at home with your wife."

"I...well I..." Bron stuttered. "If you must know, I was coming back from the tavern, I saw Ginny off on the midnight coach." He smiled thinly. "She's going to Nottingham for a few days."

Ella narrowed her eyes. That was a statement hard to prove or disprove. She glanced at the hunting bow he held, and the quiver looped over his back. "I've never seen you carry a bow and arrows."

"Well I might after that wolf attacked me last month, but nay, these aren't mine." Bron waved helplessly down the moonlit path. "I found the longbow and quiver not far back."

"How very convenient," Ella tutted.

"Calling me a liar?" Bron jabbed a finger at the black fletched end of the arrow shaft jutting from Tom's body. "It's not even the same make of arrow, see!" Tucking Tomcat under one arm, Bron swung the quiver from his shoulder and thumbed through the feathered ends of a dozen or so arrows, all identical with red and yellow feathers.

True enough. Ella gripped the head of her walking stick and hoisted herself to her feet and shook the encrusted snow from her cloak. The damp had soaked through at her knees while she knelt and now the cold seeped into her bones. "Help me move him to my cottage."

"Help a henchman?" Bron frowned. "Leave him. He probably had it coming."

"That's not for me to judge. A man's life is at stake." The baker looked about to argue further so Ella added, "Who saved your hand when you were bit by that wolf last month?"

"You did."

"And even henchmen have people who care about them, depend on them."

"Fine! But only because it's not Axel!" Bron thrust Tomcat back into her arms and without ceremony tossed aside his bow and arrows. "I'd leave Axel for the wolves!" He clasped the fabric at the shoulders of Tom's cloak and pulled the dead weight across the frozen path, grumbling as he did so.

Ella stroked Tomcat's head in a slow, deliberate manner in what she hoped was a comforting gesture, but the little cat remained limp and unresponsive in her arms.

"Did you recognise them?" she asked the baker.

"Who?" uttered Bron, puffing with the strain of part sliding, part dragging Tom's body back across the snow-coated ground towards the cottage.

"The cloaked figure."

"No." Bron gave a quick shake of his head. "At first I thought, but no…"

Ella stepped around Bron and assisted by bending back some overhanging branches. The disturbance sent a coating of snow to dust Tom's human face. But the body, like the cat, remained still and silent. "At first you thought what?"

Bron paused to stretch his back. "They wore a scarlet cloak, I thought—"

"Robinne?" Ella interjected.

"No, well Robinne…" Bron sketched a curvy, womanly shape in the air. "Nay, it's silly." He shrugged but continued, "I thought it was the outlaw, Will Scarlett, come back to haunt me."

Ella's lips thinned. Will Scarlett. The last man to openly contest Queen Sibylla's rule. The last man hanged in Wyld kingdom.

Bron adjusted his grip on Tom's lifeless body and heaved. The trees parted and they were now on the riverbanks across from Ella's home, Riverside Cottage. A welcome glow beckoned from the windows across the iced-over stream.

After dragging Tom's body down the riverbank, the baker wiped his brow. "Weighs a tonne that lad." He glanced at the white sheet of the frozen river. "Don't know the ice will take both our weight…"

Ella waved a dismissive hand. "You've done your part. I can manage from here."

"Righty-ho." Touching his hand to his cap in a salute, Bron then scrambled up the bank and into the trees without a look back in his rush to leave.

Ella sighed and hooked a finger under Tomcat's chin.

Large tears welled from emerald green eyes once so familiar and yet, now a stranger.

"Am I dead?"

Chapter 5

Frisky Pumpkins

Riverside Cottage, Wyld Enchantment Woods.

Ella thumbed the tears away from Tomcat's eyes. "I honestly don't know."

"How are we ever going to move my body all the way across the stream and into your cottage?" Tomcat fretted.

"I'll manage," Ella replied automatically, eyeing the distance from here to there and back again. Less than fifty feet give or take.

"You don't like asking for help, do you?"

"I asked the baker, didn't I?"

"What if the ice cracks?"

"Nonsense. This stream has been frozen for twenty years; the ice is a foot thick." She demonstrated this by stomping her boot on the opaque surface. "See, like a sheet of Camelot marble."

"But it's slippery, how can—"

"My boots are hobnails, I told you I'll manage." She placed Tomcat on top of his human body's legs. "Less fuss, the sooner we'll have you back in your own body and on your way."

Wouldn't that be nice?

She set her walking stick aside and grasped the edge of Tom's cloak as Bron had done. Sucking in her breath, she heaved and dragged the dead weight a foot out onto the ice.

Tomcat lurched with the movement but clung on. "Ohh, I don't like this," he wailed, staring at the black arrow sticking out of his human heart.

"Hush! Close your eyes."

Tomcat's furry little cat body hunched in, but he shut his eyes.

Ella readjusted her grip and pulled. Another foot gained. At least he slid well enough on the ice. She glanced over her shoulder. Still a good thirty, maybe forty feet, to the cottage door once they crossed the ice. And then there were the stairs up to the porch to contend with.

Tomcat opened one eye. "Need help?"

"No, I do not," Ella snapped. She wound the fabric of Tom's cloak around her hands and yanked. "Twenty years I—" she puffed between stopping and starting, "—managed perfectly fine—don't need so-called friends—nosey busybodies—interfering!"

"Sounds lonely," Tomcat said quietly.

Ella, now in the middle of the stream, stood up straight and wagged a finger. "If you think I'm going to stand here and be lectured by a mere boy who can barely hold down a *menial* job, you are sadly mistaken!"

"Hey!" Both Tomcat's ears perked up. "That's not fair, I was..." He trailed off, his feline head tilted left and right, and he jabbed a paw *look-behind-you!*

Ella glanced over her shoulder as a pumpkin vine as thick as her wrist snaked out of the night air and curled around her waist and then lifted her from her feet. "Not *me*, you big Halloween decoration!" Ella scolded the plant. "The boy, fetch the boy—gently mind!"

Tomcat leapt off his human shins as another questing vine snaked around his stricken human form and hoisted it into the air. "Careful...!" Tomcat held his breath, and then he scooted after Ella and his human body as the trailing vines receded across the stream and up the banks into the garden.

The vines set Ella down close to the porch. "Place him as far inside the door as you can," she directed.

But the plant ignored her, instead drawing Tom's body deep into the heart of the pumpkin patch where the vines began twisting and winding about him like a cocoon.

"Stop them!" Tomcat cried while Ella patted ice and plant matter from her cloak. "You said they were carnivorous!"

"That's just a rumour I spread to keep nosey people away."

"But that's so mean!"

Ella shrugged.

"You're mean!" Tomcat's ears twitched like angry triangles. "I'm starting to think you're not nice at all."

Ella's lips thinned but she held her temper. "Quit being childish and go stand in the pumpkin patch and wait for a shooting star. Then you can be on your way, and I can have my cat back."

Tomcat looked over at the rustling vines, his liquid green eyes wide and his ears flattened. "But I can't," he started to sob, "I can't go back! I'm dead, aren't I? There's an—an arrow!"

The lad had a point. Ella sighed. She wrapped her cloak tight about herself as Tomcat continued sobbing and wailing. If she shut her eyes, she could hear the pumpkins moving, rustling, as if whispering to themselves. What was it saying? Ella strained to understand the back and forth of the rustling debate when all of a sudden the plants went deathly still.

Ella opened her eyes. "Hush, lad!"

Tomcat hiccupped but managed to keep silent for a heartbeat.

—*Pop*—

Ella frowned, puzzled. A second later, a thin green vine uncoiled from the dense centre and hoicked up a long black arrow shaft at their feet.

Tomcat threw back his head and yowled.

CHAPTER 6

THE MAGIC MIRROR

WITH NO SMALL EFFORT, ELLA lowered herself, aching joints and all, to crouch down in the ice and dirt beside Tomcat. She stroked his little white head until the yowls turned to sobs and then gradually faded to hiccups.

"But why?" Tomcat sniffled, staring at the black arrow. "Why would someone shoot me?"

"I was wondering the same thing." Ella countered out on her fingers. "A robbery? A grudge? Mistaken identity."

"I don't own anything valuable. I've barely got a week's wages to my name."

"You're assuming the person knew you? A grudge then."

"No. Who would have a grudge against me? I'm super nice."

"Didn't you say you evicted a family from the cluckoo shop?"

"I didn't want to evict them! I was as nice about it as I could be—I even gave them an extra day to leave."

Ella sighed. "Let's start with robbery, assuming we believe Bron, he said the figure was searching you." She tapped the nearest vine. "Frisk him. But be gentle."

The pumpkin plant moved. Winding vines uncoiled, tendrils slipped under cloak and shirt, patted pockets and poked about his clothing. Several items were deposited in front of Ella. A coin purse. A parcel wrapped in brown paper. A horn spoon. A silver pocketknife. A copy of the *Nottingham Times* newspaper. A ticket for the stagecoach.

"Anything missing?" Ella picked up the pocketknife. It was old but prettily made, small as if for a woman's hand, with an engraved silver handle depicting unicorns.

"Everything is all there." Tomcat nuzzled her hand. "I've had that pocketknife since I was a baby," he said softly. "It was the only thing I was left with at the orphanage other than the fabric I was swaddled in."

"Uh-huh." Ella nodded but dismissed the knife. It was valuable, but not hugely so, perhaps ten golds if it was new. And not worth killing for, surely? She unlaced the purse and tipped the coins into her palm. Muttering under her breath she tallied them up. "One gold, seven silver and...sixteen coppers."

Tomcat edged closer to her and nestled down on the hem of Ella's cloak. "All there."

Ella suspected as much. A thief would have taken the whole purse. She slipped the coins back inside and nodded to the parcel. "And that is?"

Tomcat shrugged. "I don't know. It's why I was catching the coach. I'm supposed to deliver it to someone in Nottingham."

"Someone? Who?"

"I don't know, it's private business for the queen."

Ella rolled her eyes. The lad was so naive! She grabbed up the parcel and stripped off the brown paper wrappings.

"Hey!" Tomcat wailed. "That's not yours, it's not nice to be nosey."

"I never said I was *super nice*."

A flash of silver and a moment later Ella held an ornate silver hand mirror with a cracked pane of glass. Her breath caught in her throat. Ella knew exactly what the mirror was. What it could do.

Tomcat's ears dipped. "Just a broken mirror."

"Not just any mirror, a magic mirror."

"But magic is forbidden—Queen's orders!" Tomcat's whiskers fairly vibrated with indignation. "That's, that's—"

"Hypocritical," Ella finished. She turned the mirror over. A working magic mirror was extremely valuable. But a broken one? "What exactly were you told when you were given this parcel?"

"Sorry, like I said, that's classified." Tomcat mimed stitching his lips.

Ella sighed. "You were carrying something worth a king's ransom, even I'd be tempted to rob you if I'd known you were out alone with this..."

"What?" Tomcat did a double take. He leaned in close, examining his distorted reflection in the cracked mirror glass. "Hey! That's me— that's what I look like?" He turned his head this way and that. "Ohh, I'm so cute!"

"Of all the jobs, what made you pick henching, Tom? You don't seem exactly the type..." Ella struggled to find the right way to frame her question without risking further offending the lad.

Tomcat stopped batting his reflection. "I answered an advert in the

Nottingham Times. 'Are you large and good with people?'"

"Large and good with people?" Ella laughed.

"But I am good with people!" Tomcat protested. "They always do what I ask."

Ella held back a retort that people generally did what they were told when large intimidating people stood over them. There was no point. The lad had no clue that he was intimidating. Or *had* been. Now he was barely one foot tall and currently batting the glass of the mirror as it reflected light from the cottage.

"If it's magic, can it switch me back?" Tomcat asked.

"Magic mirrors don't grant wishes. They convey messages across vast distances, sometimes they herald prophecies."

"What grants wishes then?" Tomcat said thoughtfully. "Magic lamps! Let's get one of them!"

Ella thought of the lacquered box on her mantelpiece and the broken wand inside. No… There was no help coming from that quarter.

She sighed. "A magic lamp. Sure." She nudged the newspaper. "There's bound to be one in the For Sale columns. Maybe we can swap for the mirror."

Tomcat's shoulders convulsed and Ella realised he was laughing. "I didn't know you were funny," Tomcat chortled. His ears twitched, the left one dipped down and the right one flicked up. "You know what else I don't know?"

Ella arched an eyebrow and shrugged. *Where to begin?*

"I don't know your name."

"Some people call me, good mother Ella." That was true enough. Other people called her mistress Ella, or Lady Ella, and once upon people called her Princess Ella. But that had been a very long time ago…

"Good mother? Good mother?" he said incredulously. "No one says *good mother* anymore. Makes you sound like you're a thousand years old!"

Ella didn't answer. She wasn't quite *that* old. "This isn't the city, lad," she tutted. "We mountain folk hold to our traditions."

Ella had never seen a cat roll its eyes before, but she did now. "Very well, *good mother* Ella, can you make the mirror work?"

"Hello? Hello?" Ella tapped the mirror without expecting a response. Even if it wasn't damaged, this mirror belonged to Sibylla.

The chances of it working for her were slim indeed.

Tomcat started laughing again. It had been so long since she'd had company to joke with that Ella persisted, tapping the mirror and speaking loudly and slowly which made Tomcat laugh even harder.

"Hello, Mr Mirror?" she trilled. "This is your self-important queen speaking and I command your presence!"

The mirror buzzed. Ella dropped it as a jolt of light illuminated the glass.

An ethereal figure shrouded in a blue fog spoke from within, "Replaying mess—age—In W-w-wyld kingdom the reign of Sibylla ends, when—when—when—" The lights died, and the mirror silenced.

Tomcat and Ella exchanged glances. Now Ella understood why Queen Sibylla was so furious at the market last week. Sibylla's magic mirror had prophesied her downfall.

Chapter 7

Morning after the murder

The Next Day, Saturday, Riverside Cottage.

Ella spent a fitful night and woke up weary.

Eyes half-open, she lay back in warm, safe familiar surroundings: her brass bed, the feather comforter—but alas no familiar bundle of Tilly curled at the foot of her quilt—and thought over the latter part of the night before.

Firstly, the pumpkin patch had refused to give up Tom's human body, instead wrapping it in a tight shroud-like cocoon of vines. Which led to Tomcat insisting on keeping vigil outside in the cold. Eventually, Ella convinced him to perch on a chair in the parlour which she had pushed up to the window so that he could maintain watch over the garden without freezing.

And then finally, at Tomcat's insistence that there was a 'deranged murderer' on the loose, she'd locked her front door. He did have a point there, assuming the attack on him was random. But despite Ella's assurance that they were protected by the encircling pumpkin patch, nothing would allay his fears and so to keep the peace she went along with his demands and locked the door—after spending a good forty minutes hunting for a key she'd never used.

The unfamiliar noises of a stranger moving about her house brought Ella to full wakefulness and donning her patched dressing gown she went to investigate whatever that troublesome cat was up to now. Gripping the handrail for dear life, Ella's temper at the pain flaring in her knees was further riled when she heard the distinct sound of a glass jar breaking on a tiled floor. Slowly making her way down from the loft into the kitchen below she found Tomcat sweeping up the spill. He was surrounded by glass and small dark seeds scattered everywhere.

"Magic preserve me, whatever are you doing?"

Tomcat looked up from the hearth brush he clutched awkwardly in both paws; his expression remarkably sheepish for a feline. "Ahh, nuts. Did I wake you?"

Ella ignored the question and, avoiding Tomcat's mess, checked on the wood stove. But on seeing the fire was stoked she placed the kettle on top and then settled herself at the scrubbed pine table.

"Cats don't have thumbs," Tomcat said, carefully brushing the last fragments of glass and debris into the dustpan. "It makes handling things very awkward."

Ella sniffed suspiciously. An exotic scent was laden in the air. Had he put something in the oven? "What's that smell?"

Tomcat's doleful expression changed to a big toothy grin, and he sprang up onto the stool opposite. "I'm roasting seeds and herbs on a baking tray to make herbal tea for your arthritis—ginger, turmeric and black pepper." A guilty eye-dart flicked to the dustpan. "Sorry about the cumin."

Ella sat back and combed her fingers through the grey curls peeking out from under her nightcap. "I don't have arthritis," she denied. "Just a little slow to get going in the morning. Perfectly normal at my age." Not that she'd be telling him *how* old she truly was any time soon.

"Err, right…" Tomcat backed down and then nodded to the dustpan again. "You have such a wide selection of herbs and spices! I haven't seen cumin outside of Master Spicer's pantry at the orphanage."

"Is that what it's called? Que-men?" Ella sniffed. "Well, it smells nice, I admit. My sister in Constantinople sends it all to me. Don't cook with it myself."

Green feline eyes bulged wide. "Why not? Ohh—add a little cumin and rock salt and people will be lining up at the market for your pumpkin soup."

"People love my soup," Ella said, not meeting his eyes.

A small furry paw reached out across the table and pressed the back of Ella's hand. "Of course they do. I didn't mean anything."

Ella tucked her hand away. "Yes, well, let's not get soppy." She coughed. "You just caught me on a bad day…" Her thoughts drifted back to the bellowing rage of Sibylla's curses echoing about the market square the week before when she noticed Tomcat's expression, looking all horribly sympathetic like she was some foolish old lady. "I suppose it is wasteful not to use the foodstuffs Arabella sends, and learning something new won't kill me…"

She trailed off as Tomcat's little ears dipped low to what Ella had learned to recognise meant he was unhappy and realised her error.

On reflex, she glanced outside, but here at the back of the house she could see the snow-dusted apple trees, chicken coop and Tinkerbelle's barn, but not the pumpkin patch.

After a long silence Tomcat said, "I was thinking about what you said last night, the three possibilities. What about mistaken identity?"

"I ruled that one out."

"Why?"

"Because you were shot in the heart, not the back. Whoever did it saw it was you." Inwardly Ella chided her bluntness again when the little cat's ears drooped even lower.

"What about the resemblance thing?" he muttered forlornly. "I'm a lot taller, but could someone have mistaken me for Prince John? It was dark. We do kind of have the same nose."

Ella blinked. "From what I've heard, Prince John has a lot of enemies, but the chances of someone mistaking you for him is extremely unlikely given that Nottingham princes don't generally wander alone in the woods of their neighbouring kingdom." She paused. "Robbery is our most likely motive. Someone knew you were carrying the mirror. Someone good with a bow…" Her thoughts drifted to young Robinne. Robinne with her red cloak and intense dislike of the queen's regime. But surely she had no problem with Tom?

"Are you a good shot with a bow and arrow, Tom? Were you perhaps planning on entering the archery competition tomorrow?" Ella voiced as an idea occurred. "Maybe a rival thought they'd improve their chances, not knowing you were being sent to Nottingham, and you'd miss your opportunity to try and win anyway."

"I wasn't entering." Tomcat's eyes darted sideways. He wouldn't meet her eye.

"Spit it out."

He let out a breath. "You mustn't tell anyone, but Axel told me the archery competition is a cunning ploy to draw out the rebellion's leaders."

"Rebels? Hmm. There was a failed rebellion many years ago, led by a man called Will Scarlett. He wore a red cloak. Used to go by the name of the Red Unicorn while he pranced about the forest stealing from the rich."

"And giving to the poor?"

"That's the story Scarlett spread. He used to claim his arrows would miss the innocent and seek the wicked. Lies. He lined his own pockets with money stolen from rich and poor alike."

"Do you think someone could be trading on the story of the Unicorn?"

Again, Ella thought of Robinne, always dressed in her scarlet cloak and muttering sedition. Could the daughter of Will Scarlett be more than hot air?

CHAPTER 8

THAT'S NOT AN EGG

A SHARP RAP ON THE WINDOWPANE MADE ELLA JUMP. Outside a thin green tendril, the length of which was mostly coiled out of sight around the porch, swayed like a snake. The tip curled and uncurled like an index finger beckoning, *come, come.*

Now what did that pumpkin want?

Tomcat's green eyes bulged, and his fur stood on end. "Ohh no! I can't look!"

Ella lowered the drying rack hung above the stove range and retrieved her black woollen cloak. She swept it over her dressing gown and tied the ends securely. "Not knowing is worse, lad. Trust me. I speak from experience."

For a moment she thought of Richard. He had built this cottage. Not for her though, not for her. She pushed the memory aside. "Come along."

But Tomcat shook his head and stoutly refused to follow her out the backdoor, along the porch and around the corner.

Ella halted.

Overnight the pumpkin patch had doubled—tripled—quadrupled in size. A seething mass of vines six feet tall swallowed up the front lawn. And nestled among the swaying vines at the centre, a giant green pumpkin.

Magic preserve!

Ella whistled. Good gracious. It was a good five, maybe six feet in diameter. Gripping the porch balustrade, Ella negotiated the steps, one by one, down to the garden. She'd forgotten her walking stick but wasn't about to go back for it.

A wiry but strong green vine suddenly tucked under her elbow, propping Ella up, and she nodded a grudging acknowledgement of thanks at the pumpkin's aid.

Again, she could hear that strange whispering rustle as she approached. The vines dipped and bowed, brushed her face, the hem of her cloak, parting as she walked through them to the heart of the patch. The noise ceased when she reached the giant pumpkin, and she hesitated. A nudge of encouragement from her support-vine steadied her resolve. She reached out with bare hands to the pumpkin surface.

Smooth and warm to the touch.

Could she hear...*feel*...something?

Ella closed her eyes and gently pressed her cheek to the warm, green skin.

—*Da-dunk. Da-dunk*—

A steady rhythmic beat pulsed from within the oversized pumpkin. A heartbeat?

"I'm dead! I'm dead!" shrieked a voice from behind, causing her to start. "The pumpkin has eaten me!"

Magic preserve, that Tomcat will be the death of me!

Gathering her wits and hoping Tomcat hadn't seen her discomfort, Ella patted the giant pumpkin before she shuffled back toward the porch.

"No, lad, I think you're very much alive."

"What?" gasped Tomcat as he wound about her feet, threatening to accidentally trip her as she climbed the porch steps. "But the giant pumpkin?"

"That's what I'm saying," Ella replied, "I think your human body is in there, safe and sound, like a chick in an egg." She clasped the porch railing and turned back to survey her strange garden. "You're in pumpkin stasis."

"What does that mean?" Tomcat bombarded her with more questions. "How do I get out? *When* do I get out?"

Ella could only shrug. She lowered herself to sit on the top porch step, Tomcat beside her, his fluffy tail constantly flicking. Ella reached out to pet the cat but stopped herself. Tomcat wasn't her Tilly.

"Now what?"

Ella shrugged again. "I suppose we wait for it to ripen and see what hatches."

"What hatches? What *hatches*!" Tomcat repeated, his tail flicking faster than before.

"I'm sure everything will be fine," Ella fibbed.

"Has this ever happened before?" Tomcat demanded.

"Talking cats or giant pumpkins?"

"Ella!"

"It's new to me."

"I don't like it," Tomcat huffed, and sat back on his hind legs, he crossed his paws across his fluffy chest. "I don't like magic at all! I can totally see why it's forbidden." His emerald-bright eyes narrowed to green slits. "I really should report you!"

"Ohhh, should you now?" Ella mocked. "Considering the queen's strict ban on magic, how do you think she'll treat a talking cat?"

"I'll explain what happened—it's all a mix-up! I work for her!"

"That is a very foolish idea."

"You just don't want to be reported. I expect you'd find jail really hard with your arthritis."

"It's a foolish idea because someone intentionally tried to kill you last night, Tom April, and right now the only ones who know this is me, you, Baker Bron and whoever shot that black arrow!" Ella grasped the porch balustrade and hefted herself upright. "So yes, why don't you go running to the queen and see how long you last!"

"But why, why would someone try to kill me? I'm super—"

"*Super nice*—yes, I remember. And apart from your burning desire to tattle on little old ladies, you do appear to be *super nice*—if a touch annoying—so wouldn't you prefer to find out who attacked you and why?"

Tomcat's chin jutted out.

"Well?"

"And then I report you."

"Fine!" Ella flung her hands in the air. "And *then* you report me—*magic preserve me*, I'll tell the queen myself. How about that?"

"Cross your heart?"

"Cross. My. Heart." Ella drew a bony finger in a firm X over her breastbone.

"Deal." Tomcat held out a furry paw and Ella reached down, and they shook.

CHAPTER 9

HIRE A WITCH TO CATCH A KILLER

ELLA STOOD UP AND BRUSHED HER SKIRTS STRAIGHT. "While it's been nice getting to know you, Tom April, it is market day and I have a charity hospital to raise funds for, so I'll bid you good day."

"But...but...what about me? Where will I go?"

Ella tutted sympathetically. "If it's accommodation you're after, I hear the cluckoo shop is vacant."

"I can't walk around Charmington looking like a cat!"

"You should have thought of that before you turned yourself into a cat."

"I didn't turn myself into a cat!"

"I remember it quite distinctly, you stood under a shooting star and said, 'I *wish* I could trade lives.'" Ella placed a contemplative finger to her lips. "Now that I think of it...that *does* sound a lot like magic. Perhaps I should be the one to report you?"

"Haha."

Ella only smiled back. A thin small smile that said, *just wait and see if I don't.*

"Ooh, you wouldn't! Would you?"

"Tell you what, since I'm a kind-hearted, old lady, I'll let you stay in my chicken coop. We've had a spot of trouble with wolves, and I'd be glad of a cat keeping an eye on my ladies, and I'm sure Tinkerbelle wouldn't object to the company."

"Tinkerbelle?"

"My donkey. And I'm in no position to turn down a lodger."

"Lodger?"

"You can't think I'd provide *free* accommodation? Who knows how long it will take for your egg to hatch? You might be waiting here for weeks eating me out of house and home."

"But I send my wages to help Master Spicer's orphans. They need me! The tennis courts need new turf. What if I did chores instead— cut wood, um..." He looked at his two small paws. "Maybe not."

"Precisely! Now, as I was rather occupied last night, and you're distinctly going to be no help at all, I shall have to get moving if I want to prepare my world-famous pumpkin soup in time for the hungry market lunch crowd."

"But…wait, you can't mean—hold on. Do you make your soup from *that* patch?" He waved a paw to the engorged pumpkin where his human body lay entombed. "You can't feed people from those plants now!"

Ella frowned. He had a point. Kind of. "I never said my soup was strictly vegetarian."

"Ella!"

Ella put her hands on her hips. "Forgive me for being an old lady who is rather limited in her options, but like you, Tom April, I have people depending on me. My soup sales go towards the Cinderella animal hospital."

"Cinderella? Like from the storybook?"

"I have no idea what you're talking about." Ella turned her back.

"Wait, wait, good mother Ella," Tomcat called. He tugged the back of her skirt. "I'll pay you. I'll pay you for accommodation *and* to help solve my murder."

"Help you solve your murder so you can then hand me to the queen for being a witch? No, I don't think so."

"Fine, I won't report you. I promise. *Even* if *you* don't turn yourself in—like you *promised*—I won't tell anyone you're a witch." He mimed stitching his lips. "Not one word."

Ella sighed. Tapped her foot. Considered her options. "How much?"

"Huh?"

"How much will you pay me? Market day is my entire fundraising source. I can't run around trying to solve your murder *and* tend my stall."

"How much do you usually make? I'll pay double."

Ella pushed out her lips. "Very well, a dozen silvers it is."

"A dozen!" Tomcat cried aghast. "You made six silvers a day—selling that horrible lumpy goop?"

Ella cocked her head. "Are you calling me a liar?"

"Yes!"

"Well that's my price. And if you want to be out of here quicker—something I think we'd both appreciate—maybe you should sit on your pumpkin-egg to speed up the hatching process?" Ella waved a hand at the grossly oversized vegetable. "You certainly shouldn't leave it unprotected. Tinkerbelle is quite the devil to keep out of my garden, and loves to nibble on the veggies."

"Nuts! Fine. Twelve silvers."

Ella nodded. "That's what I thought." And she hobbled off to dress.

"Where are you going now?"

"What were we just discussing? I have got your murder to solve! I'll be back before sunset. If you can feed and water Tinkerbelle and collect the ladies' eggs, in between minding your pumpkin, I'd be grateful."

"You can't go wandering the woods by yourself, there's a deranged killer out there!"

"I have been wandering these woods my entire life, that's never going to change."

"No, it's too dangerous, I'll come with you."

"You're not coming to town with me." Ella wagged a reproachful finger. "All it takes is one shout from you, 'Help! Help! The witch has turned me into a cat!' And I'll be hanged in the town square before the cluckoo crows noon."

"I won't tell on you!"

"Picture it, Tom April, picture it in your mind, a poor old lady, hanging there, all the world seeing her bloomers."

"It won't happen. No one will find out, I won't speak a word, no one will suspect a thing."

"Prove it."

"Huh?"

"Act like a cat. Do something cat-like. Wash yourself."

"Err..." Tomcat rubbed his paws on his chest and started to hum.

"Not like you're in the shower!"

"Oh! Okay, I got it, look, look!" Tomcat stuck out his little pink tongue and licked one paw. He coughed and spat. "*Euurk!* Fur on my tongue!"

Ella rolled her eyes and walked away. "This is never going to work."

CHAPTER 10

ROBINNE, RUM AND RUIN

CROSSROADS TAVERN, WYLD ENCHANTMENT WOODS.

Tomcat had fallen asleep in her arms by the time Ella arrived at the Crossroads tavern. As she approached between the fir trees, her stout hobnail boots scuffing through the hard-packed snow, she could hear cheering and laughter, and on sighting the tavern and the clearing around, she spied the reason. A half dozen of the tavern's usual clientele, Dwarven gold miners, were taking turns shooting arrows at a large snowman. The snowman had a crude crown of sorts, a branch from a fir tree curled into a wreath.

Ella paused. None of the gold miners had black-feathered arrows. The majority of the arrows were fletched in yellow and green or red and yellow as the ones Bron claimed he'd found had been. Ella wondered, did the owner or the maker of the arrow decide upon the colour of the fletching?

Tomcat stirred. Pushing his chin out from the crook of Ella's arms he blinked and asked, "Why are we here?"

She set him down and pet him to whisper her reply without anyone noticing. "Three reasons. One, Robinne is an excellent archer. Two, Robinne has a red cloak."

"What?" Tomcat gasped and jumped to hide behind Ella as the backdoor to the tavern opened and Robinne herself appeared, lugging a washing basket. "You think *she* shot me? But why? She seemed so nice when I met her last week."

Ella tutted to herself. Robinne's disdain for the queen was well known—and she'd hardly been polite to Tom last week at the market despite what he said. Clearly, Tom viewed the world with a rosier glow than herself. "I hope not, but until I talk to her, I can't rule it out." Ella narrowed her eyes as Robinne walked to the clothesline and tapped the frozen line to free it of icicles. The girl wasn't wearing her distinctive cloak this morning. That was more than a little odd. Perhaps it was in the wash basket? Perhaps, last night it had become a little *bloodstained*?

Deep in thought, Ella tickled Tomcat under his chin.

"And," Tom said when Robinne disappeared back into the tavern, "what's the third reason?"

Ella patted her skirt pocket, reassuring herself she'd brought along the broken magic mirror. "I'm hoping the tavern owner, Rum, can repair the queen's mirror." She gave Tomcat a stern look. "Remember, act like a cat, say things like *meow* and not *yum, rats*."

And then, with Tomcat following close behind, she hobbled over to the washing line as Robinne returned with a pail of wooden pegs.

Ella nodded at the gold miners standing around the snowman—snow *queen*. "Any of those arrows yours?"

Robinne snorted and muttered under her breath, "Huh! As if anyone would see *me* pandering to the queen's whims."

"So, you're not going to enter the archery contest?" Ella picked up a shirt from the basket, shook it out and hung it over the rope clothesline. "I hear you're a good shot with a bow." *Like your father Will Scarlett*, Ella wanted to add but held her tongue. "And it's a lot of money."

"Whose money? She may give it out, but mark my words, she'll use taxes to pay for it." Robinne pegged the shirt on. "The people have genuine concerns; they aren't here just to provide entertainment when she's bored."

Ella smiled inwardly. How far the apple had fallen from the tree! Will Scarlett would have been plotting how to make that fat prize money all his from the moment it was mentioned.

Ella peered into the basket. Nothing red caught her eye. She shook out another garment and placed it neatly over the line. They proceeded in silence working together, hanging and pegging, all the while Robinne's teeth were chattering.

"Where's thy cloak, lass?" Ella said, exasperated by youthful stubbornness. "Go inside and fetch it."

"Couldn't find it." Robinne's characteristic scowl deepened. "Someone must have taken it last night."

"Aye?" Now that was interesting. Or perhaps a convenient lie? Ella hummed to herself. Though the girl was often loud in her views against the queen, Ella didn't think Robinne would actually go so far as to shoot one of the queen's men out of spite. Or *would* she?

"What did you think of that new Tom April? Lawks! A bit of a cutie, am I right?"

At her feet, Tomcat rolled his eyes.

"You wouldn't catch *me* with a henchman," Robinne scowled. "I can't speak for others," she added under her breath.

Ella shrugged apologetically at Tomcat. *Win some, lose some.*

Tomcat stuck out his tongue.

Ella smiled to herself. Silently relieved. Robinne hadn't reacted in a way to suggest the last time she saw Tom it was after lodging an arrow in his breastbone...

"Go in and warm yourself beside the fire," Ella told Robinne, "I'll manage the rest of your washing."

"I couldn't—"

"No arguing now, I would love a cup of your honey-bark tea and I can only pay you in trade. You wouldn't make a poor old woman beg, would thee?"

Robinne pursed her lips but stomped away, back up the steps and went inside the Crossroads tavern.

"You talk differently with the locals," Tomcat said quietly at Ella's feet.

"Lawks, do I? But I'm just an old lady from the backcountry..."

"Uh-huh," Tom replied, sounding unconvinced. "You're not like everyone else around here, don't think I haven't noticed."

"Go make use of your powers of observation over there," Ella said, nudging Tomcat with her toe, "and listen in to those men's conversations."

"What for?"

"For clues! Talk of escaped murderers. I don't know."

Tomcat muttered something and stood up on two feet.

"Act like a cat!" Ella warned between clenched teeth.

"Oops!" Tomcat immediately dropped to all fours like a regular cat, and he padded over to the small group of archers where he sat licking his paws and occasionally spitting out fur.

Humming as she worked, Ella hung the last few garments out in the crisp air. Though the sun would be bright and high today, the washing would still need to be hung above a fire to get completely dry. Such was the nature of living in eternal winter.

She recalled the brief bit of prophecy she'd heard the mirror speak the night before. If Sibylla's reign ended, so too should her reign of ice and winter. Could spring finally return to Wyld kingdom?

And maybe, just maybe, if spring returned so too would Richard...

Robinne reappeared shortly, offering a steaming cup of honey and cinnamon-scented tea.

"Thank you, dear." Ella stretched her back and wrapped her fingers around the warm, ceramic cup. She sipped while stamping her boots on the icy ground. Magic preserve, the cold seemed to seep quicker into her bones with each passing day.

Robinne noticed the gesture and motioned for her to come inside.

Ella spared a glance over at Tomcat who appeared to be laughing along with whatever joke one of the archers had said. "Aye, no, I've many errands today."

Robinne arched an eyebrow as if to say, *now who's being stubborn?*

Ella couldn't deny the truth of that. "Thank you kindly, lass, I'll just fetch my cat... Puss, puss!"

Tomcat didn't look her way.

Ella marched over, and scooped up Tomcat, who let out a startled, "Oy!"

She nodded politely at the archers, who doffed their caps and bid her, "Good morn, good mother Ella," and then she followed after Robinne into the tavern's large and functional kitchen.

When had she been here last? It was several years at least. Not long after Robinne's mother Yara passed away.

Ella sunk onto a rocking chair that Robinne dragged over beside the stove range. The fire had burned low, but the chimney and lintel stonework retained its warmth. There was a sweet aroma of yeast in the air.

On her lap, Tomcat's pink nose twitched. Likewise, Ella breathed in the fragrance. "I have a nice patch of rosemary at my cottage, you're welcome to come and help yourself—" Ella winced as Tomcat suddenly dug in his sharp claws. "Although perhaps wait a week or two, I pruned it recently." Ella settled back and sipped the tea while Robinne, resuming her chores, donned her apron and opened a door on the stove range to reveal several bowls of half-risen dough.

A ticking cluckoo clock reminded Ella of the timing of young Tom's appearance last night, roughly half an hour before midnight. If what Bron had seen was true, could the person standing over Tom's body have been wearing Robinne's cloak?

"What time did you notice your cloak was missing?"

Robinne sprinkled a board with flour and turned out a risen lump of dough upon it. "Not till this morning. It must have been taken by mistake, there are *no thieves* here." The way Robinne spoke made Ella wonder if the lass was trying to convince herself. The clientele of the tavern was a little on the rough side, poachers, gold prospectors and pedlars.

"Of course, dear, I'm sure they'll bring it back when next they're passing." Ella looked around the room. Among bunches of drying herbs, the walls were decorated with old wagon wheels and mining tools. "This place keeping you and Rum? The old road is less busy these days now they've opened the ice road."

Robinne thumped the dough hard on the floured board. "We manage." She nodded to the coaching badge pinned above the door arch. "But we have to give up the stagecoach service. The licence cost more than what we made from reservations these last three months."

"Aye, was it not full last night? The midnight coach was popular when I was a girl."

Robinne sighed. "Hardly. Aunt Ginny was the only passenger."

Ella sat up and Tomcat jumped from her lap and moved closer to watch Robinne kneading. "Oh, yes, on her visit to Nottingham."

"What?" Robinne gave Ella a look like she was crazy. "Visit?" She returned the first dough back into the oven and placed another lump upon the floured board.

Ella touched the nestled hand mirror through the fabric in her skirt pocket. "Was she well?"

"A chance to see the world..." The girl pounded on the second ball of dough. "Have her skills appreciated!"

"How's that then?"

"Aunt Ginny is taking up work in the palace kitchens over in Nottingham, she'll be head of pastries. Five staff under her and regular days off."

"But Bron said she was just going for a few days..."

Robinne dusted her hands. "You hadn't heard? She's left him— about time too."

CHAPTER II

RUM THE CRAFTSMAN

ELLA SAT BACK. Resting her elbows on the worn-smooth arms of the rocking chair, she sipped the tea. "A hard choice, leaving everything you've ever known, your family..."

Ginny was Robinne's only living relative in these parts. No doubt the girl was feeling her loss deeply, whatever she might say otherwise. Ella stood up and brushed her skirts straight. She placed the empty teacup in the sink. "Is Rum in? I need to speak with him."

Robinne motioned to a doorway. "Upstairs in his workroom."

"Come along, Cat, we'll leave Robinne to her tasks." Ella patted Robinne's shoulder as she passed. "And I'm sure once Ginny is settled, she'll have you around for a visit. Maybe I'll go too. My sister Arabella keeps asking me to visit her and Nottingham is on the way."

"DOES YOUR SISTER ARABELLA LIVE IN NOTTINGHAM CITY?" Tomcat asked when they were alone in the hallway.

"No, Arabella works in far off Constantinople," Ella said, contemplating the steep and narrow staircase up to the loft above the tavern's main common room.

Stairs! So many stairs. If she ever got her magic back, she was never going to walk up another flight of stairs again!

"Master Spicer is from Constantinople," Tomcat added, bounding light-footed up the stairs, two at a time. "This is a strange staircase. The steps are much smaller than normal."

"Rum is small. Remember your manners when we're in his workroom and don't stare at him," Ella responded while holding the handrail tightly to keep herself steady.

And to think she had momentarily worried last night that *she* might have traded bodies with Tom—that would have been a welcome respite from this frail old body.

"How many sisters do you have?" Tom sat on the top step, waiting for her to catch up. "I always wanted a sister. Or a brother... Did you have any brothers?"

"I have two sisters living, one passed, and one brother, also very much alive and rather full of himself." Ella momentarily thought of her brother Merlin—*full of himself* barely scratched the surface, he was a smug old goat.

"Three living siblings... Wait. Are they *all* as *old* as you?"

"Just when I was starting to like you," Ella puffed, having reached the top of the stairs. "Now hold your tongue and think cat thoughts."

"Cat thoughts?"

"Like whether you prefer rats or mice."

"I'm vegetarian!"

"Of course you are... Now, hush!" She knocked on the door at the top of the stairs and called out, "Rum, it's Ella. Are you free? I have a sensitive problem requiring your unique skills."

A gruff voice replied, "Enter."

Ella gave Tomcat one more warning to stay silent by tapping a finger to her lips and opened the door into Rum's workroom. The loft space, built in the rafters of the tavern overlooked the main common room below, served as both office and workroom. Filled with Rum's accounts books and half-finished projects the room was a feast for the eyes. The inner workings of a cluckoo clock, rows of wood carving tools, leather punches, wood shavings, bundles of arrows, and many miniature carvings of wolves and unicorns.

Rum looked up from his desk, a whittling knife in one hand, a block of wood in the other. He brushed some shavings from the leather apron he wore.

Tomcat's eyes went from the tiny wee man and his gaze only widened as he gaped at the treasures littered about the workshop. "Whoa! Did you make all this awesome stuff?"

"Tom?" Ella let out a long sigh. "What did we discuss?"

"Oops," said Tomcat, clamping a belated paw to his mouth. "I mean, yum, rats?"

Ella only shook her head. "Rum, despite evidence to the contrary, Tom isn't the problem."

"Aye," Rum said, setting the carving aside, he flexed his wrist which was bound with a strip of linen. He pulled his shirt sleeve down over the bandage when he caught Ella looking. "Dinnae worry, is nay but a small...lesson in economics."

"At whose hands?" Ella demanded.

Rum shook off her concern. "Dinnae worry yourself. The queen likes to assert her authority every now and then."

"Hmm, via Axel no doubt?" Ella tapped a toe.

"Axel?" Tomcat sat back on his haunches. "I thought he was nice."

Rum laughed again. "You're a funny wee fellow, Axel nice? Aye, nice of him to concern himself with my health, aye indeed."

Tomcat folded his arms across his chest. "You don't seem concerned by talking cats," he said and hitched a paw at Ella. "Are you a witch, like Ella?"

Rum laughed. "Mistress Ella's nay a witch! That much I know." He shared a look with Ella as if to enquire *how much* she'd told the cat about herself.

Ella gave a quick shake of her head. Drawing an empty crate over to act as a stool, Ella settled upon it. "What do you know about arrows?"

"I can make them if that's what you're asking." He nodded to a selection of arrows with yellow and green feathers like the ones being shot into the snowman outside. "By the dozen. Naturally. Good quality, not like that cheap rubbish sold in town."

"Do you know a fletcher who uses black feathers?"

Rum looked away; his bottom lip jutted out in a facial shrug. "Not that I recall. Ahh, entering the queen's competition, are you? Robinne was all innae state about that last Saturday afternoon, came an' demanded I cut her bowstrings."

"And did you?"

"As if I could—It'd be a crime to damage a bow like that. I just hung it up on the wall out of the way until she calms down..." He nodded to an empty space on the wall. "Ah, that's odd now, so it is, was there yesterday. Perhaps the lass changed her mind. Thousand coins, a lot of money, so it is. I've half a mind to try for it meself in all." He rubbed his wrist thoughtfully.

"It might be best if you don't compete, I hear the queen is using the competition to draw out the rebellion's leaders."

"Rebellion? What rebellion?" He clasped a hand over his linen bandage. "No one who remembers the dark days is foolhardy enough to cross the queen."

Ella arched an eyebrow.

He shook off her implication. "Young Robinne talks a great deal, holds her meetings and the like, but it's just kids blowing off steam."

Ella lowered her voice, but Tomcat was paying their conversation no attention as he was engrossed in playing with the collection of miniature wooden unicorns. "Does Robinne know she's Will Scarlett's daughter?"

Rum shook his head. "Robinne's mother Yara and I—Creator rest her bones—kept the truth from the lass, to keep her safe. Not even Yara's sister Ginny knows." He leaned back in his chair. "How's an archery competition supposed to expose rebels, tell me that now?"

Ella reached into her pocket. "I was hoping you could tell me." She drew out the magic mirror.

"Hey!" Tomcat said, putting down a carved unicorn he had been making kiss another figurine. "That belongs to the queen!"

"Yes, and like I told you, Rum might be able to repair it," Ella responded. "Don't you think that would be nice? Put you in her good books?"

Rum sat up straight, the whittling knife clenched. "The cat works for the queen?"

Tomcat blanched but Ella replied, "No, no! The cat is mine."

"No, I'm not!" Tomcat interjected. "The cat is his own man."

Ella held back a smile. The cat was no man at all. "Can you repair it?"

Rum swallowed. "I told Axel I could nay."

"Axel?"

Rum nodded, looking pale. "Aye, a few days ago, he came to see me. He did nay say it was the queen's mirror, but I knew..."

Ella nodded. "Worth a king's ransom."

"Aye." He coughed. "Sometimes the lad brings me things to repair, I've a mind he sells them after... So, when I spied the mirror, well, I wanted none of it. I told him outright."

Tomcat tilted his head. "You're not trying to suggest Axel was stealing it? I'm sure he just wanted to repair it to please the queen."

"And *could* you have fixed it?" She offered Rum the mirror.

"I shouldn't even be touching it—Queen will hang me." Despite this protest, Rum opened a top drawer and pulled out a magnifying loop which he placed to his eye. He slid open a panel at the back of the mirror. "Aye, for sure, crystal array is out of alignment. Did somebody throw this against a wall or the like?"

Ella shrugged. She could well imagine an enraged Sibylla hurling the mirror.

Something went *ting* and the blue light once more beamed out of the glass. The voice Ella had heard last night immediately spoke up, "*Replaying message. In Wyld kingdom the reign of Sibylla ends, when the unicorn walks free and spring returns with long-lost friends.*"

The colour drained from Rum's face and the loop fell into his lap.

"Ohhh, was that a prophecy? That was neat!" Tomcat leapt up onto the desk. He pressed a paw onto the mirror. "Play it again, Rum."

Ella nodded. "Yes. Play it again. Do you have a pencil? I'll write it down."

Rum shook his head emphatically. "I think you should be going. I can nay be mixed up in rebels—Queen keeps an eye on me." He raised his bandage wrist. "As well ye can see."

"*Message deleted.*"

"Oops," said Tomcat. "Did I do that?"

Chapter 12

Marge the Midwife

RUM THRUST THE MIRROR BACK into Ella's hands and then ushered her and Tomcat from his workroom quick-smart, practically slamming the door in their faces the moment they were both out in the hallway.

Ella returned the mirror to her skirt pocket and felt around the lining. There were a few pumpkin seeds, but nothing else. "Do you have a pencil? I want to write the prophecy down before I forget it."

Tomcat made a rather dramatic show of patting his furry body before replying, "No. Technically I'm naked."

Ella rolled her eyes.

"Where to next?" Tomcat asked as Ella made her way slowly and steadily down the staircase.

"Town, we'll catch a goodsbarge travelling the ice road. I want to go to the cluckoo shop and see how those tenants feel about you evicting them."

"But I was nice to them!" Tomcat protested as they walked through another doorway and into the tavern common room below.

Ella shrugged. "Eviction is a sound reason for a grudge."

The large and usually welcoming room was nearly empty, the few people that were there were all crowded to a window, their faces pressed to the glass they gawked outside at something occurring out on the porch.

Ella scooped Tomcat up and opened the door onto the front verandah where Robinne was engaged in a rather heated exchange with a short, tubby woman with a bunch of blonde curls peeking out from under her midwife's bonnet.

Ella sighed. The midwife, Marge, was a newcomer to the area, having only lived in Wyld kingdom for the past three years. A notorious gossip, she was never backward in coming forward.

"It's a public notice!" Marge was saying, waving a sheet of paper on which something was written about a book club. "Therefore, I don't have to pay to display it."

"I don't care what your notice *says*, it's not a public noticeboard,"

Robinne countered. "It's the tavern noticeboard and it costs a copper to post notices!"

"Why didn't you just say so?" Marge said loudly, looking to Ella as if for support.

"I did!" Robinne replied just as loudly, and then she pointed to the neatly hand-painted lettering at the bottom of the sign stating the rates and conditions of using the noticeboard. "And it's written here—just as it was the last time you tried to cheat us."

"Well really," Marge huffed, backing down, "there's no need to be rude."

Ella tried to shuffle past the pair and escape but on seeing her chance to likewise escape, Marge laced her arm into the crook of Ella's and guided her down the porch steps.

"Heavens, let me escort you, Lady Ella, whatever are *you* doing in such a *rough* establishment?" The last part of her sentence Marge directed back at Robinne. And then the midwife pushed her notice into Ella's free hand. "No doubt you'll be interested in this book club, being a culturally-minded woman like myself?"

Ella had been about to refuse the notice when she had second thoughts and could see how handy it was to suddenly have been given a free piece of paper. "Lawks. Yes." She smiled winningly. "Is there any chance you also have a pencil?"

Marge reached into a pocket inside her short cape. The lining was red. A bit flashy for Ella's tastes and alas no pencil was stashed within, but she did offer to assist Ella to the edge of the ice road from where she could catch the barge to Charmington township. Marge might be an awful gossip, but she had a steady arm and for once Ella was interested in all Marge had to offer. If there were rumours of deranged murderers on the loose, Marge would know.

As they walked the gravelled old road Marge broke into laughter and nodded slyly. "She might well be cross," Marge said with an artful look over her shoulder, back at Robinne who was still out on the tavern porch and ripping down other notices from the board. "Her and all her high ideals."

"Beg pardon?"

"Miss Robinne, salt to the wound." Marge patted Ella's hand as if they were in complete understanding of each other.

Ella spared a glance to make sure Tomcat was following behind. He was and, even better, he was slinking along on all fours. For all the world looking every bit like a regular cat.

"I really have no idea what you're talking about." Ella folded the book club notice into her skirt pocket with the mirror and hoped someone on the goodsbarge might have a pencil. Already she was forgetting how the prophecy went exactly. Something about unicorns and spring...

"Well, really, you must be the only one! Everyone's talking about it. You know that handsome new guardsman?"

"Yes..." Ella replied, glancing down at Tomcat, who puffed out his chest and strutted along the path ahead of them, his cat-slink turning into a prance.

"Guess who's gone and run off with him?" Marge cocked her head back towards the tavern, her cherub expression devilishly gleeful.

"Who?"

"Ginny! Robinne's aunt—Robinne was spitting tacks over it last night. Ranting this and that about the queen like she always does." Marge sighed longingly. "Can you imagine? A handsome young man, sweeping you off your feet! So romantic."

Ella gaped down at Tomcat who sat in the middle of the road and waved a not-so-subtle paw, cutting the air in an *I-did-no-such-thing* gesture.

"Let me see if I follow," Ella questioned the midwife. "You're saying Ginny—Baker Bron's wife—has run off with Tom April the guardsman?"

"Uh-huh."

Tomcat shook his head. *Nuh-uh.*

"And where did you learn this juicy bit of gossip?"

"Goldilocks told Cheapcuts the butcher's boy, and he told Katie the milkmaid, and she told me."

"Goldilocks—the queen's hairdresser—told Cheapcuts the butcher's boy—who last week told everyone a wolfman ate his lunch—told Katie, the I-like-a-sly-drink, milkmaid turned barmaid?"

"That's right." Marge beamed. Her blue eyes and blonde curls were a deceptive picture of sweetness, like a dimple-faced cherub with a heart of coal.

"Then it must be true." Ella looked back at the tavern, now nearly out of sight among the fir trees. "And this affected Robinne? She wasn't pleased."

"Spitting tacks—Katie's exact words. Apparently, Miss High-and-

Mighty turns her nose up at decent, hard-working men. A bit rich coming from someone who doesn't know who their father is, if you ask me."

"I didn't, but there you go."

Marge sniffed. "Well excuse me for living."

Ella patted Marge's hand and smiled. "If only I could, my dear, if only I could."

Chapter 13

Catching a Goodsbarge

Ella and Tomcat were soon on their way to Charmington having caught a passing goodsbarge. They settled among barrels and boxes as the converted boat glided along the frozen river on sledge fins.

With a pencil from the kindly bargeman, Ella wrote down the prophecy as best she remembered:

> *In Wyld kingdom Sibylla's rule ends, when the*
> *unicorn is free, something something, spring blooms*
> *and brings friends.*

"Is this what you recall?" she asked Tomcat quietly, with a glance at the barge owner at the tiller. But the man, bundled up under a layer of scarves and coats, paid her no attention, all his focus was fixed on making sure the boat's sail caught the wind and carried them efficiently down the frozen stream.

Tomcat's ears flicked up. "I've always wanted to see a unicorn."

Ella tutted. "That's not going to happen."

"Aww, why not?"

Ella gestured to the passing snow-shrouded forest. "You're thinking too literally. There haven't been real unicorns in these woods for hundreds of years. But *The Red Unicorn* was what the outlaw Will Scarlett called himself when he pranced around causing trouble. It's no wonder Sibylla suspects a rebellion. That's what the mirror's prophecy suggests to me also."

"So you think the Red Unicorn person could return?"

"Will? No. He was hanged." Ella thought back to something Bron had said last night. Hadn't he said something to the effect of Will Scarlett coming back to haunt him? That was an odd turn of phrase. Why would Will haunt the baker of all people?

"It's just I overheard Axel and the queen discussing Will Scarlett."

"Really? When?" Ella hunkered down and tugged her cloak hood about her neck. No wonder the bargeman was so bundled up. The wind chill was frightful.

"Early last Saturday morning. Before the market opened. The queen was very upset. I was waiting in the hallway while she spoke with Axel. She said, 'Am I never to be free of Will Scarlett?'"

"That's the same day she announced the archery contest..." Ella tapped the pencil to her lips.

"Yes, Axel suggested the archery contest because, quote, 'Will could never resist the chance to show off his skills or make money.' So, he must be alive. They want to catch him."

Ella shook her head. "Will Scarlett is dead. Ask Axel, he was the executioner."

"Oh." Tomcat's ears dipped low, and he was silent for several minutes. "Do you think Axel *deliberately* hurt the craftsman, Rum? Maybe it was an accident."

Ella sighed. Poor boy, he wanted to see the best in everyone. It made him blind. "Ask yourself, did Axel hesitate when telling you to evict a family from the cluckoo shop? No, because Axel is used to doing Sibylla's dirty work."

Tomcat's little body hunched inwards. "Doesn't mean he likes doing it."

"Your experience is limited, wait until you've seen his typical, heavy-handedness and then decide. But think, what if someone local has had enough of Axel's bullying ways and decided to strike back? Maybe they even thought it would send a message that the only good henchman was a dead henchman?"

"Huh? Do you think Axel might be targeted too? We have to go warn him!"

Ella rolled her eyes. No, that hadn't been her point at all. "I'm sure Axel can take care of himself. Aside from the evicted family, is there anyone else you can think of that we need to talk to?"

"You need to go tell the queen you have her mirror."

Maybe. Maybe not. Ella tapped the pencil to her lips again and surveyed the collection of parcels and crates that filled the deck of the little boat. It did raise another question she had been pondering. "Why didn't Sibylla have Axel take the mirror to Nottingham? Why give it to you?"

Tomcat shrugged. "I'm from Nottingham, maybe she thought I'd enjoy the trip. And like you say, it's valuable. I was extra protection."

Ella had the good grace not to mention how well his extra protection worked out as she mulled this over. "Sibylla could have easily sent the parcel via the postal service. I think she was worried the prophecy might keep replaying and someone not loyal to her would hear it."

"You are going to give the mirror back to her? Right?" Tomcat flexed his little claws into the sack of potatoes he rested on.

"Well..."

"Ella!"

"I think we do need to send it on its way, certainly. Someone is probably expecting it." Ella moved a parcel that was digging into her spine.

"Good."

"See, that right there—you're trustworthy. Sibylla was right in giving you that task. Just as she knows which tasks to give Axel."

"Unpleasant tasks," Tomcat muttered.

"Hmm..."

"Now what are you thinking?"

"Beyond the monetary allure of the mirror, maybe someone else desperately wanted to hear that prophecy? Maybe Sibylla has suspected a rebellion before this prophecy confirmed it last week."

Tom cocked his head. "Maybe someone *was* acting on Will's memory. A new Red Unicorn!"

"Someone who also wears a red cloak..." Ella sighed. That thinking pointed her back toward Robinne—who theoretically didn't know Will Scarlett was her father...but what if she did? Ella thought back to the market day a week ago. No... Robinne had appeared as oblivious to the queen's agitation as Ella herself. Of course, the lass could have found out any time after the market about the prophecy.

Ella tutted to herself, clicking her tongue, but pencilled in *Suspects: evicted family* and *Robinne*.

Tomcat batted the paper. "No, c'mon, you still don't believe that nice girl can have anything to do with this?"

"I don't know what to believe," Ella admitted. Then she perked up as another idea occurred. "What if someone expected you on that coach? Someone who knew you had the mirror. Maybe they were going to wait until you fell asleep on the journey and pick your pocket? But when you didn't turn up, they went hunting for you... Who else knew you were catching the coach?"

"No one, the instructions said it was top secret, even from the castle staff."

"Wait, your orders were written? You didn't speak to anyone?"

"Er... I shouldn't have said anything. It's classified top secret!"

"Tom! How do you expect me to help if you don't tell me things? Didn't it occur to you that *anyone* could have written that note? They might have been *using* you to deliver the mirror straight to them."

"Oh no!" Tomcat cradled his whiskers with both paws. "I'm an accessory to theft!"

"Calm down, we can't draw any conclusions yet..." Ella thought back over the gossip Marge had spread. "What about Goldilocks, did you meet her while you were at the castle?"

"I don't think so. What does she look like?"

"Four feet tall. Bouffant hairdo. She's one of the wee folk, like Rum. She's a part-time hairdresser—once upon a time safecracker—and as the name suggests, very good with locks. She could definitely pick your pocket."

Tomcat shook his head slowly. "I don't think so."

"Shame. Marge did mention her. Never mind."

He looked sideways. "Ohh! But the instructions are still in my room! We can get them—and then, and then, compare handwriting samples from *everyone* in the castle!"

"I like the first part of that plan..." Ella contemplated trying to get handwriting samples from that many people without causing suspicion. She didn't foresee that going well. "And on the way, let's stop by the Gatehouse Inn and see if they have a master list of coach passengers for last night. Maybe you and Ginny weren't the only two who had tickets."

CHAPTER 14

I LOVE SUSHI

The Gatehouse Inn was precisely as the name suggested, an inn located on the main thoroughfare just beyond the northern gatehouse into the town of Charmington. In Ella's youth, outdoor tables adorned with red and white check tablecloths fronted the establishment. Crimson and scarlet geraniums overflowed from flower boxes under the lead glass windows.

Eternal winter had done away with the flowers and forced the diners and tables all inside. But the atmosphere was still familiar and welcoming.

"Ooh, I love the Gatehouse Inn, they do an excellent vegetarian lasagne and the desserts!" Tomcat chatted as they approached. "Perfectly caramelised maple and walnut pie! Follow that with their decadent full-cream hot chocolate and you have a superb lunch."

"I'm not sure Arthur would serve cats…"

Tomcat's ears dipped. "Ah right. I forgot."

"But if you can keep quiet, I'll sneak you a hot chocolate under the table." Ella scraped the snow from her boot soles while Tomcat waited patiently on the steps. "Tom, I'm going to ask the proprietor, Arthur, a few provoking questions about you, so remember to stay silent no matter what you hear me say. Agreed?"

Tomcat nodded.

The voices and aroma of fresh bread, venison and rosemary stew, spilling from the inn took Ella back. She could easily imagine she was here to meet her sisters and share a table with their friends, to spend an afternoon drinking ginger beer, eating cakes and gossiping over books and boys.

Ella sighed and chided herself. Her youth was gone. Her friends were gone. Ginger beer made her gassy. She peeled off a glove and lifted the door latch. Tomcat darted in, hiding behind her skirts.

They needn't have bothered with the subterfuge. Arthur, the proprietor, a retired guardsman who had worked for the castle since boyhood stopped wiping down the bar and swept her up in a warm embrace.

"Mistress Ella! How long has it been? You've made my day!"

He escorted her over to a table for two near the fireside and beside a lead glass window overlooking the comings and goings out on the cobbled square. And then he scooped up Tomcat and placed him on the other red velvet seat and chucked his chin. "Who's a good pussycat? Yes, you are! I have a nice piece of fish for you, yes I do." And then to Ella, "Ginger and carrot soup? Lemon tea?" Barely waiting for a response, he called for his assistant Katie and dashed off into the kitchen.

Ella bowed her head, eyes fixed on the handwritten menu at the table, waiting until the other half dozen diners were once again focused on their own meals and conversations.

Arthur was back in a moment, a silver platter in one hand, a red and white cloth in the other. He placed the platter, laden with a plump salmon fillet dressed with cream and sprigs of dill, in front of Tomcat, then deftly tied the cloth around Tomcat's white neck.

"Sushi!" Tomcat said, licking his lips. "I love sushi…" He froze when Arthur did a double take and several diners looked up from their soup bowls, spoons held aloft like figurines whose cluckworks had wound down and were frozen in mid-action.

"Oh dear," muttered Ella, staring down at her white knuckles, laced together over a crisp linen napkin across her lap. She should have asked for more money! At this rate the lad would get her hanged before nightfall.

Tomcat's ears flattened to his head. Clearly ashamed. Poor lad. He was too open and honest. And if Sibylla hadn't banned magic, he'd be an amusing curiosity rather than dangerous contraband that might get people locked up or worse.

"This is a rare Macaw cat," Ella said loudly, addressing the gawking onlookers, "they can be taught to mimic phrases, just like parrots."

"Indeed, as soon as I saw him," Arthur replied, "said to myself, why, there's a fine example of a Macaw cat."

Arthur placed a tender hand on Ella's shoulder and gave a gentle squeeze. Ella nodded in silent understanding. That she would ever try to endanger or be endangered here was unthinkable. And perhaps she had been wrong too, to assume all her friends were gone.

Arthur looked around and nodded encouragingly at the blank-faced customers. "Perhaps…a gift from your sister who works for the sultan himself in faraway Constantinople?"

A thin man with a pale ginger moustache, who had been reading a book and eating an egg salad sandwich at the bar, and whom Ella recognised as the new school teacher, snapped his book shut and said, "My aunt had a Macaw cat who could recite Tennyson."

"My…my grandmother had a pig who could count to ten!" added another diner. An elderly lady bedecked in ribbons and bows, sitting with her sister, likewise attired in flounces. They owned the haberdashery across the square. What were their names? Millie and Sally.

Ella breathed out as the atmosphere relaxed, eyes were once again averted, spoons clanged and middle-class conversations and dining resumed.

Arthur gestured to the wood-panelled staircase. "Would you prefer the private dining room upstairs?"

Ella frowned at the stairs. "No, thank you, Arthur. I'm sorry for the fuss." She gave Tomcat a stern look, although she suspected he'd be as quiet as the grave for the rest of the meal.

Arthur dismissed her concern with a cheery smile and fetched her soup. After waiting to watch Ella have a taste he asked, "Anything else I can get you?"

Ella recalled her purpose. "Do you still take reservations for Hansel and Gretel's midnight coach?"

Arthur nodded that he did. "Planning a trip? Visit Arabella?" He grinned broadly.

Ella lowered her voice. "I just need to know who bought tickets for last night." She subtly nodded to Tomcat who was daintily eating his raw fish. "A bit of confusion I'm trying to help sort out."

Arthur nodded sagely. "Aye, a lot of confusion swirling around today." He turned his gaze to the direction of the castle and tapped his nose. "Whispers there's been a sighting. Of a certain… Unicorn."

Ella set her soup spoon aside. "Unicorn?"

Arthur pointedly touched the panel of red velvet backing on Tomcat's chair.

Red velvet? Red? Did he mean Will Scarlett, aka the Red Unicorn?

"Speaking of recidivist troublemakers," Ella added, "I heard the family from the cluckoo shop were evicted yesterday. Axel's doing?"

"No, the new lad, Tom April, comes in here most days—he was

telling me about a spicy soup recipe using curry and coconut."

Ella pulled a face. Coconut soup? That didn't sound like a thing. "I suppose you won't be serving him now he's shown his true colours—tossing an innocent family out on the street in winter."

Arthur scratched his head. "Oh, well, Tom's a nice young man, no one has a bad word to say against him. Well, until the er...Ginny thing. But that's just gossip."

Ella arched an eyebrow and Tomcat grinned ear to ear.

Arthur coughed. "I'll fetch the coach register."

Ella frowned and helped herself to more of the fragrant soup. Thick and chunky, ground barley, slices of carrot, a hint of ginger with a swirl of cream. She savoured every delicious spoonful. Arthur must have learned the recipe from his grandmother. Or perhaps his grandmother's grandmother. Ella frowned. The townspeople changed so frequently. Like the new school teacher. At least the haberdashery twins—Millie and Sally—were familiar faces, though faded like their ribbons. Ella recalled the day they were born one hundred years ago. Or was that the day Arthur's grandmother was born? She peered over at Tomcat, seemingly happy munching on his cold fish. Odd idea. Raw fish. And didn't he say he was vegetarian? "Is that actually nice?" Ella said aloud. "Cold, raw fish?"

Tomcat stopped eating. But didn't answer. As if he was being tested.

Ella just nodded, as if he'd passed her test, suddenly guiltily aware she had slipped up herself. Keeping secrets wasn't easy.

"Here we are," Arthur said, returning to the table with a fat old leather-bound ledger. Ella gestured for him to sit with them, and he pulled over another chair and flicked through the pages. "Dear, oh dear," he muttered, tracing a finger over the columns and rows of names. "The ice road has really been bad for the stagecoach business, fewer passengers every month. I haven't looked in here for ages, Katie handles all the bookings. Her handwriting is so much neater than mine..." He tapped the last entry. "Here we are. Ginny Bron. Ticket for two."

"Two? Er, meow!" Tomcat suddenly said.

Ella narrowed her eyes at him. Tomcat's tail flicked rapidly, and he pawed at the tabletop.

Ella gave him a nod to acknowledge she saw his signal. "Ginny Bron?" Ella voiced. "And she was going to the city of Nottingham with someone, not alone?"

"Aye," Arthur replied, glancing at the ledger. "Ahh! Speaking of travel, how's Arabella doing? Magician to a sultan! What an achievement. You must be proud."

"Er, right." Ella looked down.

"Each to their own path, of course," Arthur blustered as if sensing he'd put his foot in it. He stood up suddenly, ledger tucked under his arm. "Goodness, I've forgotten your tea—I'll be right back!"

Ella focused on her soup, purposefully not making eye contact with Tomcat whose tail hadn't stopped flicking. Tomcat leapt on the tabletop and sat directly in front of Ella.

Tomcat whispered, "Your sister is a magician?"

"Well..." Ella stalled. "Technically no. Over there they call her a genie."

"Ella, you swore you're not a witch." His green eyes narrowed to slivers. "What are you then?"

Ella looked around. But the dining room had cleared, momentarily they were alone. "I'm retired, that's what I am, thank you very much."

She tried to nudge Tomcat aside, but he put his paw on the back of Ella's hand, pinning her soup spoon to the bowl. "Ella, what were you before you retired?"

Ella sighed. Time to come clean. "Once upon a time, I was a fairy godmother."

Chapter 15

How Ella lost her wand

"Say that again?"

"A fairy godmother. I was a fairy godmother."

"What? You mean a fairy godmother with a wand, grants wishes, turns pumpkins into coaches, that sort of fairy...ooh!" Understanding dawned in Tomcat's eyes. "Pumpkins..."

Ella raised her eyebrows. "Indeed."

"What happened?" Tomcat leaned closer. "Why'd you give it up?"

"I was audited by the Fairy Council." Ella shut her eyes and thought of the box on her mantelpiece containing the two halves of her broken wand. "They discovered I had been granting wishes for...for myself." She took a deep breath, opened her eyes. "It's not allowed. I was de-wanded." She mimed the snapping of her wand.

Tomcat winced. "I'm really sorry to hear that."

Ella shrugged. Looked down. "It was my own fault," she mumbled, "I broke the rule."

"Sounds like a stupid rule!" Tomcat huffed. "Why shouldn't you be able to grant wishes for yourself?"

Ella shrugged again. What could she say? "Please just know, even though magic is forbidden, if I had my powers, I'd try to turn you back into a person."

Tomcat pressed his paw lightly to the back of Ella's hand. "Never doubted it."

Ella looked away and blinked back tears.

"And it could be worse—what if you had a pet snake or parrot? I much prefer being a cat."

"Why would a parrot be so bad? Then you could fly."

"Exactly! I am afraid of heights!"

Ella knew he was joking, just trying to be nice. But she managed a chuckle.

"Ahem," Arthur coughed politely from the doorway into the kitchen, alerting them to his presence. "Service for the lunch crowd starts shortly," he said, coming over to their table. "You're very welcome to stay, but it does get busy."

Say no more. Ella knew precisely what he was implying. Not everyone in Wyld kingdom could be trusted to hold their tongue about talking cats...

Ella pushed her chair back and scooped Tomcat into her arms. "No, thank you, Arthur. We'll—*I'll*—be going. Thank you for your hospitality."

"You're always welcome here, Mistress Ella."

As SOON AS THEY WERE both back out on the frosty cobbled square, Tomcat prancing at her side, Ella brought up the clue Tomcat had been trying to signal. "What were you trying to signal me about Ginny?"

"Huh?" Tomcat stopped prancing and looked momentarily confused, but then his eyes went wide. He cocked his head *follow-me* and ducked down an alley between the haberdashery and the cluckoo shop.

"Ginny Bron!" he hissed when they were alone. "Ticket for two."

"Yes...? You think whoever she was travelling with attacked you?"

"No! Maybe, I don't know." Tomcat slapped a paw to his forehead. "But why wasn't *my* name on the register? I had a ticket for the coach."

"Did you purchase it?"

"No, it was with the parcel and the instructions I found in my room."

Oh, really? Now that was interesting. Had Ginny bought the ticket for Tom?

"We need to see those instructions." Ella looked towards the castle. "Do you think you can go fetch them while I talk to Bron at the market?"

Tomcat nodded. "Sure, but remind me why you're talking to Bron again? Didn't you believe him last night?"

"Truth be told, I did then. But Robinne was muttering something about people dating henchmen, and Marge's gossip about you and Bron's wife—"

"Which is not true!"

"Undoubtedly, but rumours spread quickly, clearly Arthur had heard it. What if Bron also heard the rumour? Hmm?" She arched an eyebrow, nudging Tomcat to mentally join the dots. "Are you forgetting who we found standing over your body?"

His little mouth fell open. "It can't have been the baker—he seemed genuinely upset."

Ella hummed. "True... But Bron told us a lie. He said Ginny was away on a short trip. Implied she would return home. Why?"

"Maybe he was heartbroken that she'd left him and couldn't face telling strangers. Who knows?"

"I'm not a stranger! But I can sympathise that he'd want to avoid the nasty gossips." She took out the book club notice and added Bron to the top of her pencilled list of suspects.

Tomcat's ears perked up. He stretched his body, placing his paws up onto the wall of the cluckoo shop building. "What's that noise?"

"I don't hear anything..." Ella began, but then she did. The crunch and snap of something wooden being smashed.

Tomcat darted off down the alley towards the shop front entrance before she could stop him.

Chapter 16

Axel Puts the Cluckoo Shop Out of Business

Cluckoo Shop, Northgate Square, Charmington.

A crowd had gathered at the entrance of the shop and Ella had to elbow her way through the spectators as chairs and other various bits of broken furniture were hurled from the doorway to litter the street.

Avoiding the gawkers, and flying housewares, Ella entered the shop to find Axel and a harried-looking woman with a wailing baby on her hip and a brood of miserably thin children clutching her skirts.

"Please, you don't understand, my husband has been ill—his chest!" the woman was begging Axel as he carried a tin bath to the doorway. "He hasn't been able to carve the little roosters!"

"Pay your rent!" Axel brushed Ella aside and chucked the bath, scattering the crowd as it bounced and clanged on the cobbles. "And you can stay!"

"But yesterday the other man said we could return for our belongings once we find a new place!" the woman protested when he came back inside.

"Yesterday, *smesterday*, promises get broken all the time—get used to it!" Axel looked around the workshop.

The woman stood in front of a workbench full of hand tools and blocked Axel. "Wait, please! My husband can't work at all without his tools!"

Tomcat darted between their feet. "Leave her alone!" Tomcat yelled, hissing and rising up on two legs.

"Good grief!" Axel aimed a kick. "Harbouring magical creatures! That'll get you hanged!"

The woman and her children wailed as Axel chased Tomcat out of the room and down the hallway, deeper into the building.

"Quickly," Ella instructed, waving the family out of the workshop, "take refuge at Arthur's, go while you can!"

"But the tools!"

"Take what you can carry, go, go! I'll keep him busy," Ella said, and then ventured further into the shop. She spied Axel swiping at a flash of white leaping for a small open window in the back.

"Did you hear that?" Axel peered out the window into the alley beyond and then glanced over his shoulder at Ella. "A talking cat!"

"That wasn't the cat you heard, you fool," Ella blustered, trying to sound bolder than she felt. "That was me! Talking cats! What a load of nonsense."

Axel made a noise of disgust and tried to push past her to get back to the shop area, but Ella stood firm and blocked the narrow hallway. "Out of my way, Granny," he growled, "I've Queen's business to attend to."

"I just had a question, er..." Ella racked her brain, trying to think of how to stall him, "...about the archery contest tomorrow."

"What? You?" He laughed. "Are you going to enter—you look like you're made of twigs! Can you even draw a bow?"

"I'll have you know," Ella stuttered, heat rising to her cheeks. "I was an excellent shot as a girl."

"Hate to be the one to tell you," Axel countered in a low voice, looming over her, "but you're long past being a girl."

"Ooh!" Ella blurted, her ploy to stall him forgotten as her temper flared. "You! If I... Ooh! How rude!"

"Move aside, Granny, or I'll—" Axel suddenly grasped Ella about the waist, lifted her and deposited her behind him in one smooth, effortless motion.

"Mercy!" Ella clutched her chest, her heart racing as Axel stormed off down the hallway. Shaken, she leaned against the wall. That was a very unpleasant dose of reality. Why, he seemed to find the effort of lifting her no harder than she might find lifting Tilly. Was he really that strong? Or worse...she that weak?

"Argh!" Ella flinched back as Tomcat suddenly jumped in through the open window.

"Is he gone?" Tomcat questioned.

Ella shook her head, and waved her hand down the hallway, momentarily unable to speak.

"Are you okay?" Tomcat was pulling one of his sympathetic faces, head tilted, ears dipping. "He didn't hurt you, did he?"

"I am perfectly fine," Ella replied more tartly than she intended. "Wait for me out in the alley, and for heaven's sake, learn to hold your tongue!"

Tomcat's head drooped. But he nodded.

Ella swallowed hard and pushed off from the wall. She marched down the hall, telling herself, *I am not a helpless old lady, I am not a helpless old lady!*

"I still have questions," Ella demanded of Axel as he proceeded in his destruction of the family possessions by putting a foot through a child's doll house. "About the contest, I need some arrows. They are very expensive. Tom April said he could loan me some."

"Tom?" Axel said over his shoulder as he swept ornaments from the mantelpiece onto the floor.

"Yes, he speaks highly of you."

"Quit wasting my time."

"Have you seen him today?"

"What?" Axel paused, boot hovering over a ceramic dove that hadn't broken in its descent from the mantelpiece.

"I asked where Tom is this morning."

Axel grinned. "Ha! Haven't you heard? Young Tom April has run off with Ginny the baker's wife!" His boot came down, smashing the dove into smithereens.

Ella exited with as much dignity as she could, her heart pounding.

Tomcat was not waiting for her in the alley behind the cluckoo shop. Worried, Ella looked around. Where could he be? Hiding?

"Puss, puss," she called tentatively while peering down the icy cobbled path.

Two bright red drops of blood marred a patch of snow.

Magic preserve. Now what trouble had befallen Tom?

CHAPTER 17

HABERDASHERY TWINS TO THE RESCUE

"Yoo-hoo! Lady Ella," called the shrill voice of an older woman. Ella stood up straight to see one of the fraternal twins who owned the haberdashery and had also been at the Gatehouse Inn that morning. She was trying to attract Ella's attention by waving a white lace handkerchief from where she stood on the back porch of the neighbouring building.

Which one was she? Sally or Millie?

"Millie is tending your precious Macaw," the ribbon-bedecked lady—Sally—explained as Ella walked across the narrow pathway and followed her into the lavender-scented backrooms of their haberdashery. "Poor darling has cut a paw."

Tomcat was perched on a large cutting table among scissors, bright scraps of cloth, half-trimmed bonnets, and silk flowers. A linen bandage tied neatly on his front paw. Millie, dressed to match her sister in emerald green with white polka dots, was fussing with a candy-striped scarf which she tied in an elegant bow about Tomcat's neck.

"Ooh! Doesn't she look darling, sister dear, you have such a deft touch with bows!" Sally exclaimed, clapping her hands in delight.

Millie inclined her head while plumping the bow. "Lady Ella, there you are, we knew you must be nearby." She gestured for Ella to take a chair beside Tomcat.

Ella sunk into the chair and closed her eyes briefly.

"Lady Ella, you're so pale!" Millie exclaimed. "Whatever is the matter? Fetch the smelling salts and put the tea on, would you, sister dear?"

"I'm fine," Ella soothed. "Just..." Flustered? Perhaps, dare she even admit to herself, a little frightened.

"It's that horrid henchman, Axel," Sally answered on Ella's behalf, jabbing a finger in quite an unladylike fashion towards the neighbouring business.

"Don't fret, your precious pet is in good health." Millie patted Ella's hand reassuringly. "I have cleansed and dressed the wound, just a small cut."

"Splinter," voiced Tomcat holding up his bandaged paw. His eyes bulged as he caught Ella's stern gaze. "Oops."

"Oh! How charming!" Both haberdashery twins cooed and tickled Tomcat's chin. "Say something else. Who's a clever puss?"

"Wherever did you get a Macaw cat?" Millie asked, fussing with the bow affixed about Tomcat's neck while Sally failed to coax more words from Tom.

Thankfully.

"Just my good fortune," Ella replied thinly. She should have known bringing him into town was a mistake. The lad was going to get her hanged long before she figured out who had attacked him. She was starting to have some sympathy for the 'deranged murderer'. Tom was more trouble than first appearances would lead one to believe.

"Such a sweet face! Will you put him out for stud?" encouraged Millie, draping a floral garland on Tomcat's head.

"Now there's a thought," Ella said with a smirk at Tomcat's sudden wide-eyed look of horror. She drummed her fingernails on the smooth oak tabletop. "I certainly wouldn't be opposed to selling him, should you ever be in the market."

"Oh, how can you joke about this sweet boy?" Millie laughed, stroking Tomcat's head. "Don't listen to your mean mummy!"

"Don't be silly, sister, it's clearly a girl." Sally nodded at Tomcat and wagged her little finger. "No er...baubles."

Millie grimaced. "Sister! Don't be vulgar!"

"What the...?" said Tomcat, staring down at his furry tummy, he patted his body and Ella bit her lip and looked away.

A sheet of paper on the table caught her eye—the notice for the book club. Had she dropped it? Wait, no... The momentary concern she'd dropped her list of suspects faded away as she realised it was another copy.

Sally saw her reading the notice. "Do say you'll come along to our club! Millie and I were just discussing this month's book only last night, weren't we, sister? Show her, show her."

Millie frowned, apparently not sharing her sister's enthusiasm, but fetched a thin pink book tucked between two bolts of lace on a shelf.

The book was titled *Cinderella* and had an impossibly beautiful woman in a voluminous silver dress, running down a castle staircase. She pressed the book into Ella's hands. "You're welcome to borrow it, but it's probably not your cup of tea. Just remember, it's only a story."

A story? About Cinderella? Hadn't Tom said something about a Cinderella story? Surely it couldn't be about *her* sister Cinderella, though. Could it?

"It's just a bit of fun—" Sally ceased chattering suddenly as her twin gave her a stern look.

Tomcat leaned over. "I've read this..." Then meeting Ella's eye he likewise trailed off into reproachful silence with Sally.

"I think that must be my cue to leave," Ella said, pushing back the chair from the cutting table and scooping Tomcat up under one arm. She set the book down on the table but hesitated. Truly, it was more than a little unsettling to see her dead sister's name emblazoned on the cover, but surely that was where the coincidence ended.

Ella tucked the slim volume into her skirt pocket alongside the mirror. "Thank you for your kindness, I assure you, you'll be first in line to receive one of the kittens."

She didn't need to look to know that Tomcat was rolling his eyes as the sisters clucked and fussed over him, tickling his chin as they escorted her to the door.

"Your scarf?" Ella said, pausing on the threshold.

Millie waved her off. "Keep it, she looks darling!"

Ella smiled her farewells and waved over her shoulder as she set off down the icy lane, with Tomcat whispering in her ear, "When were you going to tell me your cat is female?"

CHAPTER 18

TO MARKET, TO MARKET TO BUY A FAT PIG

MARKET SQUARE, CHARMINGTON.

"Did you remember to warn Axel?" Tomcat asked quietly as Ella carried him, navigating her way through the frozen streets towards the market square. She nodded to people she knew who in turn, depending on how well they knew her, either smiled, or the older, more formal among them, doffed their caps or made a quick bow or curtsey.

"Warn him about what?" Ella replied, thinking back on her unpleasant encounter. She had known Axel was a bit heavy-handed, but never had she witnessed his temper up close. Even though not directed at her, it had left her more than a little unsettled. Left her feeling...? Helpless. Frail. Old.

"About the deranged murderer targeting the queen's men!" Tomcat insisted.

"No," admitted Ella, walking across the covered bridge into the market square where she paused. The weekly market had been forced to the very edges of the square as the central area was crowded with people practising archery on a set of improvised butts in the form of a row of hay bales.

Magic preserve, that was dangerous!

In a crowded market a stray arrow could cause a nasty accident. Despite this possibility, the dangling carrot of a thousand gold coins was overruling common sense and the townspeople seemed only too glad to queue up to take a turn at the butts. Ella cast her eyes across the arrows being used. No one had black fletched arrows.

Hmm, that was both good and bad. Good because it suggested that when they did find the user of the black arrows, they'd surely have their man, but bad in that presently they were no further along in ascertaining who that individual might be.

"Why not?" Tom continued in a loud whisper.

"Because," said Ella, surveying the stalls that had managed to squeeze in and around the practising archers, "I don't believe there is a deranged murderer. You were chosen for who you are or what you carried." She peered this way and that. Where had Bron set up his bakery stall today? She could not spot it among the jostling townsfolk and vendors. "Now hush, help me look for Baker Bron."

Tomcat made a sigh but otherwise held his tongue while Ella elbowed through the line of waiting archers to the nearest stall, the butchers.

"Greetings, your ladyship," the butcher's wife, Martha, a rotund woman, said, having removed a clay pipe from her lips, and jetted a warm tobacco cloud into the chilly air.

The butcher, a beefy man with a grizzled beard and the hairiest arms Ella had ever seen, was less attentive. Appearing distracted he banged his cleaver down on the cutting board, embedding it upright. Wiping his hands on his blue and white striped apron he nudged his wife who spoke aloud, "Aye, Chelton my love, there's our boy now."

Ella turned to follow the couples' gaze to see their son, Chelton junior, better known as Cheapcuts, a scruffy lad of indeterminate age, who had been somewhere between nine and fifteen for the past decade, all elbows and knees as another growth spurt made his clothes and appearance even more gangly than Ella last recalled. Cheapcuts, at the head of the line of archers, nocked an arrow and drew back on an ancient hunting bow, the wood creaking audibly despite the distance separating them.

Mother and father held their collective breath as the arrow loosed, soared, and *thunked* into the top right hay bale of the target—two over.

Both parents sighed and tutted. Martha nodded to her husband Chelton, as if to say, *Told you*, but then turned her rosy smile back on Ella. "Can I tempt thee with a side of bacon? Honey smoked?"

Ella was about to decline when a small, sharp elbow thumping her ribs and Tomcat's nodding face peering up at her, licking his feline lips, made her hesitate. Odd, hadn't he said he was vegetarian? Although he had chowed down that fish... But regardless, meat was expensive, bacon even more so, she seldom bought it. Then again, Tom had agreed to pay her twelve silvers—essentially he'd be paying for it.

"Can you deliver?" Ella asked cheerily and was met with positive assurance and jokes about the boy delivering it tomorrow after the grand archery contest unless by a miracle of fortune Cheapcuts managed to win, and then Martha herself would deliver it by sleigh pulled by a unicorn in a silver harness.

"Where is Baker Bron set up today?" Ella enquired of the couple as the Saturday crowd flowed around them.

Martha exchanged looks with Chelton who abashed, drew breath between clenched teeth.

"Not here, I take it?" Ella said, studying their expressions. Behind Martha's back, Chelton mimed raising a bottle to his lips, but Martha caught him and slapped his hand away.

"Under the weather, poor fellow," Martha replied with fake joviality.

Ella nodded grimly. *Understood.* Bidding them good day she wove back through the crowds towards the castle wall on the far side of the market square.

"Now where to?" Tomcat asked as Ella ducked around the noticeboard and passed by an argument between two rival shoeshine stands competing for the prime spot.

"As Bron hasn't brought the bakery to the market, we'll take ourselves to his bakery."

"But that's *way* across the other side of town!" Tomcat voiced. "I'm already concerned for your knees."

"Very kind," Ella replied drolly, "but fortunately I know a shortcut. *Through*, rather than around the castle!" She waited for a cart to cross the bridge and then set off along the covered walkway at the base of the castle when among the various tones and textures of brown and green cloaks a flash of scarlet caught her eye.

"Tom!"

"I see it!" Tomcat said aloud. "Follow them!"

CHAPTER 19

THE SUMMER GARDEN

CHARMINGTON CASTLE.

Destination forgotten, Ella laboured to catch up with the red-cloaked person in the distance, but the crowds of market day combined with the archery hopefuls clogged up the path.

Tomcat struggled in her arms. "Set me down!"

But Ella clung on tighter as the swarm of townsfolk bumped into her. "No! You'll be stepped on!" In vain she hobbled after the flash of scarlet, but in a moment they were gone and Ella sagged against the stonework at the base of the castle wall.

"You should have let me go after them!" Tomcat grumbled.

Ella pushed off from the wall and backtracked towards the market. "And let my Tilly be crushed under a boot or cartwheel? You forget your size." With Tomcat muttering in her arms, she veered down an unobtrusive archway off the main covered walkway and stopped in front of a stout oak door bound with iron studs.

"That's definitely locked," Tomcat uttered, but craned upwards from her grasp to have a better look as Ella clasped the large latch. The heavy door swung open on groaning hinges.

"WHERE ARE WE...?" Tomcat whispered a moment later as they continued down a narrow stone corridor that opened out into a beautiful walled garden courtyard. Fragrant jasmine grew up the walls, there was a pond, a small fountain and a row of blossoming cherry trees, all the more delightful for being free from any traces of snow.

"Ohh..." Tomcat breathed in wonder as Ella gently set him down onto the marble tiles laid out in a pretty swirling mosaic. He padded to the edge of the pool and gazed into the water. "Hey, no ice! How's that possible—hey look, there's a big turtle!"

Ella wasn't surprised by the summer garden, it had after all been a great favourite of all the sisters when they were children, but the turtle was news. She joined Tomcat at the pool's edge and peered down into the shallow waters. Through the pink and blue flowering water lilies, among the darting goldfish with long flowing fins of orange and white, was a large green turtle, gently sculling along the bottom of the pool, investigating the pebbles and lily roots with his beak.

"How old do you think he is?" Tomcat said, leaning even closer. "Is it a turtle or a tortoise? He's massive!"

Ella could only shrug. Turtle or tortoise she knew nothing of the differences between, just as she couldn't begin to guess as to the creature's age. He hadn't been here when she last lived in the castle nearly two decades ago. Sibylla must have added him to the pond since then.

The sound of a door closing across the garden behind the cherry trees made her look up. Sibylla stood there; her lustrous chestnut hair pulled back into a pert ponytail. She wore a figure-hugging outfit in emerald green, consisting of a tunic and men's breeches, a narrow peaked hat with a long red feather, for all the world looking like some kind of bizarre cross between a page boy and a sharply dressed huntsman.

"Magic preserve me!" Ella found herself saying before she could stop. "What *are* you wearing?"

Sibylla smiled, stood on tiptoe and did a quick twirl. "It's very becoming, isn't it? I will be the talk of the town tomorrow." She touched her hand to her breastbone, her head tilted back as if she were imagining the sighs and stares her grandiose presence would elicit.

Something about Sibylla's posing, her odd fancy costume and due to Ella also sighting an archery target set up in front of the roses at the far end of the garden, set an alarm bell *tinkling* a warning in Ella's mind. "Tomorrow?"

"When I win the contest of course," Sibylla muttered, a sly smile illuminating her perfect features, making her expression sharp like a fox. "You can't think I'd give up a thousand gold coins without a fight?"

Ella crossed her arms and glanced down at Tomcat, but he was pawing at the water's reflection, for all the world acting like a real cat entranced by the darting goldfish. "But if you compete, you'll put people off from entering," Ella voiced tartly.

"Exactly the point," Sibylla returned smoothly. "Only a disloyal rebel would dare show up their queen." She picked up a hunting bow that was on a table laid out with cakes and other dainties. "Won't you come and take a shot?"

"No, but I'll spare a few minutes to watch you miss the target," Ella returned, warming to the idea. She recalled how dreadful Sibylla had been with a bow and arrow as children. "After all, I'm probably the only one who dares clap when you miss."

"Oh, you're so mean." Sibylla laughed and made a coy, one-shoulder shrug. "I rather think I'll surprise you with how much I've improved, sister dear."

Uh oh! Had he heard? Ella glanced down at Tomcat.

Tomcat's ears perked up, he turned to Ella and she could see the word *"Sister?"* forming on his whiskers, so she hurriedly looked away to avoid one potential awkwardness only to see Sibylla pick up a quiver full of arrows. Black arrows.

CHAPTER 20

MIRROR, MIRROR

SIBYLLA WINKED AT ELLA, NOCKED A BLACK ARROW TO HER BOW, drew back and loosed. The arrow hit the bullseye dead centre.

"I don't believe it," Ella said, heart racing, struggling to comprehend the larger meaning of what she had just witnessed. Sibylla's arrows looked exactly the same as what young Tom had been shot with.

"I told you I've been practising," Sibylla gloated. "Shall I demonstrate again? Even with my eyes closed, I hit where I aim. Every. Time."

"I don't believe it," Ella repeated as another black arrow struck true. Was Sibylla the murderer? But why, why shoot Tom?

"That's your pride speaking." Sibylla shrugged and stooped to pick up a third arrow from the quiver. "That's always been your problem, too proud to admit when you're in the wrong."

Ella clutched her cloak, drawing it protectively close to her throat, as she gaped at the quiver full of black arrows. Could it be true? No, it didn't make sense. Tom had been sent on a secret mission by Sibylla, entrusted with an extremely precious treasure, a magical treasure worth more than he'd ever make in his lifetime. What was to be gained by killing the one person honest enough to protect that treasure?

How many, how many? A deep part of her brain was tapping the back of her eyes, trying to get their cooperation. Rum had said something about arrows being made by the dozen.

"Eleven!" Ella blurted, scanning those shafts remaining in the quiver plus the two already in the target and the one in hand. One arrow was missing from the set. "Magic preserve me, it's true. It could have been you! But why?"

"What are you blathering about, sister dear?" Sibylla replied calmly, setting the bow down and pouring herself a cup of tea from the table laid out with enticing luncheon treats.

"Tom! Kind-hearted, loyal, Tom!"

"Are you having a senior moment? This is what comes from only having chickens and a donkey to talk to…" She poured a second cup and motioned for Ella to take it. Sibylla's smile was cooler than ice and twice as slippery. "Your old chamber is exactly as you left it, all you have to do is publicly admit that Cinderella's tragic death was entirely your fault, and all is forgiven."

The rebuke might as well have been a slap. Ella was jolted by the sudden sting of old blame. "Me? My fault?"

"Like I said," Sibylla tutted wearily, "too proud even to do the right thing."

"Of all the hypocritical things to say!" Ella dug her hand into her pocket, fingers closed about the silver hand mirror and she offered it up. "Why give him the mirror and then try and kill him?"

Sibylla thumped the delicate china cup down, eyes now flashing with anger. "Where did you get that? Are you stealing from me now?"

"You deny you gave it to young Tom?" Ella retorted and cast a glance over at the turtle pond, but Tomcat was nowhere to be seen. Had he run off on discovering they were sisters, or had he also recognized the significance of the black arrows?

"Tom who?" Sibylla replied quietly, brows furrowed. "Certainly, I deny giving it to anyone, I didn't know it was missing." She snatched the mirror and ran a thumb over the cracked glass.

Ella blinked, swallowed, suddenly unsure. Sibylla sounded more genuine than Ella had heard in a long time. Was she telling the truth?

And worse, Ella realised with dawning horror, had she wanted Sibylla to be guilty? What kind of person, what kind of sister did that make her?

"I have to go…" she mumbled. "I… I just came to return the mirror."

Sibylla only nodded, but then called out as Ella walked away, "Take care of yourself, sister, I worry about you. All alone in the woods. It's a dangerous place."

CHAPTER 21

HUNT FOR TOM

ELLA HURRIED AWAY DOWN THE NEAREST CORRIDOR, deeper into the castle, quite unaware of destination or purpose, her turbulent mind filled only with the sight of the black arrows—eleven black arrows!

Didn't that prove it? One arrow was missing! Sibylla was the owner of the black arrows; she must have been the one who shot poor Tom! There was no other logical conclusion. But why? Why do it?

Her feet sought the east tower staircase of their own volition, seeking the safety and comfort held within her suite of rooms which lay long forgotten at the top of the tower.

"Are you lost, grandmother?"

A kindly voice, attached to the scrubbed-clean face of an earnest-looking servant girl, perched at the foot of the staircase railings, broke through Ella's mental distress and confusion.

"Me?"

The lass wrung out the polishing cloth she'd been wiping across the balustrade. "Only the dairy is on the far side of the main courtyard?"

Spoken like a question, the girl's innocent statement had Ella clap a hand to her lips to stop a curt, *Don't you know who I am?*

She shook off the nettled pride, of course she looked more like she belonged in the dairy than the ballroom. She nodded. "Thank you, my dear, forgive an old woman, I got turned about."

"Oh aye, it's easy enough to be sure," the bright young thing replied cheerfully, "I got frightful lost my first week here."

Ella could not voice her reply, just touched the lass's shoulder and walked back the way she'd come, following the servants' passageways. This grand set of buildings had once been her home. Every night she had closed her eyes, secure in her place and right to be here as had generations of her family. Perhaps Sibylla was right, was it merely her pride keeping her out? Charmington castle was her home, her birthright.

Ella could not accuse her sister of neglecting the place. Every windowpane gleamed and every piece of brass shone bright like a mirror, reflecting Ella's withered features. She looked away.

Where was everyone? These halls usually bustled with the many people required to keep the castle maintained and running smoothly as cluckworks.

On opening a side door out into the main internal courtyard, Ella had her answer. Every rank of servant, from highest to lowest, bootboy to butler seemed gathered out on the frosty cobbles, and like the common people who flooded the market square beyond, their attention was fixed on watching guardsmen and other hopefuls practising their archery skills. Arrows fletched in bright colours, greens, reds, and yellows, flew through the air to cheers and good-natured jeers alike.

No black arrows...

More proof of Sibylla's involvement? Ella shook her head, dismissing her thought. Despite past grievances and hurt, and while she may not entirely trust her sister, there was one truth she could not deny. Sibylla was no fool. She would not waste the loyalty of an honest man like Tom, she might well wring every drop for herself, but she would not squander it! A man like Tom was more useful to her alive.

Hands on hips, Ella stood on the edge of the gathered servants, peering this way and that, and then cast her gaze down at milling feet, scanning the ground for a flash of white fur.

Magic preserve! Where had Tomcat run off to? And had he seen the black arrows too?

Ella tapped a hobnail boot and hummed. If she were young like Tom, frightened and upset, where might she hide? Where might he seek comfort? What did she know of the lad's likes and dislikes? Food, yes...and animals...perhaps?

The clouds of steam from the breath of laughing and jostling people in the wintry air all around gave her an idea. The stables! Yes, of course, he'd likely go pat a horse, away from the noise.

The stables were just across the courtyard and as most corridors within the castle lead to the central courtyard it seemed as good a place as any to try.

Ella entered the stables a few minutes later and was greeted with a pleasant change in temperature as well as old familiar smells of hay and leather, and the gentle nicker of the horses. Surely Tomcat would be in here somewhere? She paused to scratch each horse between their ears as she went from stall to stall, softly calling out Tom's name.

No luck. Now what? Could he have climbed up into the hayloft? Tilly would have. But Tom? Was he thinking as a man or as a cat?

Ella frowned at the tall and rickety ladder up to the hayloft. She definitely would not be attempting to climb that. "Tom?" she called in a loud whisper and then waited, straining her hearing for any telltale rustle from the straw above.

Nothing.

The horses stared at her with their large wet eyes, blinking impossibly long eyelashes. Once she knew every beast stabled here, but now, like the servants outside, they were all strangers to her.

Where would Tom go?

Ah! She had it, of course! Chiding herself for overlooking such an obvious answer when she had automatically followed such a path minutes before, Ella exited out through the back of the stables and into the warren of low connecting buildings that made up the quarters for grooms and lower guardsmen. Tom would have sought out his own room!

Deep in her thoughts, Ella hurried around a corner and collided hard with another person. They clunked skulls and then bounced off each other in a tangle of limbs.

"Ouch!" The other person clutched their forehead. "Watch where you're going!"

Ella blinked, stunned and confused, at the familiar face. "Ginny!"

Ginny Bron, the baker's wife, reached out a hand and hauled Ella to her feet. "Good mother Ella, what are you doing here?"

"I might ask the same of you." Ella straightened her clothes and probed a finger to her throbbing forehead. "I thought you left on the midnight coach. You should be halfway to Nottingham by now."

Ginny cast a guilty glance behind her, drawing attention to a door chalk-marked *April*. "I was..." Ginny said hesitantly, "but the coach broke down, lost a wheel, and it was forced back."

"Were you in Tom's room?" Ella pressed, suspicions raised.

"Of course not!" Ginny cast another guilty look at the nearby door. "But you do know who I mean? Tom April?"

"Certainly, Axel's good friend."

Axel's *good friend*? Ella leaned closer.

A thin smile suddenly flashed across the baker's wife's face. "Tom mentioned he worked for a wheelwright last summer and I thought he might be able to help Hansel and Gretel work on the wheel repair to speed things up."

Ella frowned. While that sounded perfectly reasonable, it wasn't as if Hansel and Gretel would need any such aid. Despite their apparent youth, the two millennials were far stronger and older than anyone Ella knew.

"Why don't I walk you out?" Ella folded her arms. "I'm sure you'll be in a hurry to spend your final time here with Bron."

Ginny blanched, but then pulled a wide confident smile betraying that Ella might have just overplayed her hand. Ginny laughed softly. "You don't know anything."

With that enigmatic gloat, Ginny stomped off, leaving Ella alone to contemplate. Whatever Ginny was hiding, at least she seemed to think Tom was alive. Clearly, she was hunting for him.

Well, Ella had the advantage there, she knew what shape to look for...

Ella pushed on the door marked *April*, it swung open.

Gracious! What a mess! Bedding on the floor, drawers open, contents in disarray. Did Tom live like this?

Ella caught herself. No. Of course not.

Tom hadn't made this mess, Ginny had. She hadn't been looking for Tom, she was looking for something he had—hadn't Bron himself said the person in the red cloak was searching Tom's body? But then again that in itself didn't make sense. Why would Bron risk betraying his wife...?

A faint noise made Ella start. She held her breath. There it was again...a sniffling...?

"Are you under the bed, Tom?"

"No," came back a sulky voice from under the bed.

Ella sighed. She pulled the blankets back into some semblance of order and perched on the bedside. "Are you crying?"

"No." A pink nose pushed out from under the bed frame. Tomcat shook his white head. His large green eyes were glossy with tears, his candy-striped silk scarf limp and dishevelled. "Maybe."

Unthinkingly, Ella reached out and scratched behind his ears. "It's been a tough couple of days."

Tomcat disappeared back under the bed.

Ella stood up. "If you want to stay, that's your decision, but I had better get moving. I've Tinkerbelle and the chickens to think of, I can't leave them alone all day." She paused at the doorway.

No response from under the bed.

"I sure hope I make it home before dark."

No response.

"I sure hope I don't run into the wolf that bit Bron last month."

No response.

Ella sighed. Magic preserve, it had been a rough couple of days indeed.

"Tom, did you find those instructions?"

The tip of a pink nose reappeared. "No, Axel's girlfriend, Ginny Spicer, came in so I hid under the bed."

Chapter 22

Top Secret Instructions

"Say that again?"

Tomcat crept out from under the bed. "I had just got here when Axel's girlfriend—"

"Axel's *girlfriend*?" Ella blinked incredulously and hooked a thumb towards the hall. "That woman who just came in?"

Tom nodded.

"I don't believe this." Ella shook her head and sunk down onto the bed. "Ginny is Axel's girlfriend. Are you sure?"

"What?" Tomcat tapped a paw against Ella's knee. "What's wrong?"

"That was Ginny Bron—Spicer was her maiden name! She's Bron the baker's wife!" Ella cast her mind back to Robinne's bitter comment about people seeing henchmen. It was too awful to comprehend. The man who executed her father, dating her aunt. "And you're sure she's Axel's girlfriend?"

"I'm *almost* certain. I only saw them together a few times and Axel told me to keep my nose out of his business. But I overheard them discussing travel plans, they were planning to go away together."

"Then why didn't you say that earlier?"

"Ginny's a common name—the baker's surname is Bron, I just didn't make the connection!" Tomcat's ears dipped. "And Axel, chase after a married woman? I never thought..."

Hmm, well Ella wasn't at all surprised. Not by Axel's behaviour. She'd often observed Axel ogling Ginny at the weekly market. She was surprised however that Ginny didn't have better taste. Still, love was blind. Apparently.

Tomcat looked up. "Do you think Ginny shot me?"

"Er..." Ella hesitated. Did that mean Tomcat hadn't seen Sibylla with the set of black arrows? She patted her pocket and drew out the pencil and book club notice. "I can't think why she would, but I guess we can't rule it out."

She added Ginny's name to the suspects' list. *Robinne. Bron. Ginny.*

There was a definite connection between the three of them. *Niece. Uncle. Aunt.* But what connected them to Tom? With the pencil in hand, she rolled it back and forth across her fingertips, deep in thought.

Should she add Sibylla to the list?

She couldn't deny what she'd seen. The black arrows were the only clear clue to the person who attacked Tom, and that pointed directly to Sibylla. But what was her possible motive? Then again, what could these others have against Tom?

A spark of memory reignited a theory. Marge the gossiping midwife claimed Ginny had run off with Tom, and she wasn't the only one to say that, both Arthur and Axel mentioned it. If Bron had also heard the malicious gossip then that certainly gave him a motivation of jealousy. And Robinne's dislike of the queen's regime was well-known. But what motivation did Ginny have? The ransacked room suggested she was searching for something. Had she somehow known about the magic mirror that Tom carried and was planning to rob him?

Ella stood up and thrust the pencil and paper back into her skirt pocket. "We have to go talk to Bron. Are you coming?" She walked to the door without looking back and was pleased to find that Tomcat trotted after her.

"Wait! The instructions!" Tomcat called, coming to a screeching halt, he ducked back into his sleeping quarters to return a second later with a piece of folded parchment in his mouth.

Ella relieved him of the burden and unfolded the paper to read, in Sibylla's neat handwriting: *Task for April. Deliver to Nottingham Palace. Guard with your life. Tell no one.*

"Well, it's Sibylla's handwriting, that much I can confirm." Ella studied the instructions. There was something not quite right with the paper. Something she couldn't put her finger on...

"Knew it would be," Tom said smugly. "I knew she trusted me. I'm one-hundred per cent loyal to the queen."

"That's so comforting to know," Ella said drily, refolding the note and tucking it in her pocket. "Do you think Ginny saw this?"

Tomcat shrugged. "Probably. It was on my desk."

Ella rolled her eyes. "Magic preserve me, Tom!"

"What?" Tom yowled back as Ella stomped off down the corridor muttering to herself.

Why would Ginny leave the instructions behind when she had the opportunity to take them? Then again, written in Sibylla's handwriting, the instructions couldn't be connected to Ginny who didn't even work in the castle. Once again, another clue that pointed back to Sibylla…?

"Hey, are we trying to catch up with Ginny?" Tom asked when they ventured out of the sleeping quarters, behind the stables, passed the dairy and through a side gate back into the township.

"I don't know where she went," Ella admitted, scooping Tomcat up from the path as the rumble of cartwheels and booted feet threatened to squash him. Ella cast her gaze on the people going about their daily business. Most were dressed in black, brown or green. Sombre, practical colours. If only they'd caught up with the person in red!

Ella paused to listen to the cluckoo clock chiming from the town hall tower in the distant Northgate square. "But if we go talk to Bron I expect Ginny will cross our paths again. The stagecoach is located next door to the bakery."

Chapter 23

Hansel and Gretel

"You're going the wrong way. The bakery is that building there." Tom jabbed a white paw toward the three-storey stone building, set a little back from its neighbours in Southgate square.

"I know but I'm going into the tavern because it's between the bakery and the coaching stables, and the Chelton's implied Bron had been drinking..."

"I don't think you should go in." Tomcat dug his claws into the icy cobbles. "That tavern looks rough."

Tom had a point. The Huntsman tavern had certainly seen better days. Located just within the south gate, the once-grand old building had lost its lustre and its clientele as use of the forest road dwindled once the ice road became the main thoroughfare into the township. Surrounding businesses relocated to the northern side of town or closed down. Only the neighbouring bakery, stables and butchery remained in operation, less easy to relocate due to their machinery and size.

The Huntsman tavern had suffered in other ways too, more than just loss of foot traffic. A year ago, a fire had ripped through the top floor. The damage hadn't been repaired, the upstairs windows were all boarded over, and much of the upper stonework was still blackened.

But Ella knew appearances were deceptive. The Huntsman had a very loyal patronage, many of whom like her were of a much *older* set.

She gave Tomcat a wink. "Keep your eyes open, you might spot a juicy rat. Yum!"

"That's not funny!" Tom said, scampering at her heels to stay close when she pushed the door open.

Ella blinked as she entered the gloom within. No daylight entered the Huntsman. By design.

Tomcat tugged the hem of Ella's cloak. "Can we please go," he whispered, surveying the dark interior. At the bar, no large mirrors served to help reflect the melted stubs of candles nestled atop yellowing skulls from assorted animals. Wolves, horses, large birds of prey, and even human skulls, grinning with gap-toothed animosity, were stacked between rows of ancient green bottles sulking under a layer of dust.

"What are you complaining about?" Ella said with a shrug. "I like it. It's got an atmosphere."

"Atmosphere of death," Tom muttered as they edged through the empty tables and chairs towards the tall bar where Bron the baker was slouched on a stool, asleep within a veritable forest of shot glasses, wine bottles and beer mugs, his face smooshed to the countertop.

The swing door behind the bar into the kitchen swooshed open. A pretty little blonde pigtailed girl in a blue denim dirndl skipped up to the bar, hopped up on a box or step located for her use, and set a tiny, multi-faceted, crystal bottle on the counter.

"*Scheisse!* Is Highness!" the little girl cried, spying Ella, and clapped her hands to her face in apparent surprise or joy.

"Gretel," Ella acknowledged with a nod.

Gretel turned her head and bellowed over her shoulder, "Hansel! *Dummkopf!* Bring buttocks here! *Schnell!*"

Ella in the meantime levered herself up onto a barstool beside the snoring baker. Tomcat, lithe footed, sprung up onto the counter and navigated through the assortment of bottles and glasses.

"Ah! Kitty!" Gretel squealed, scooping Tomcat towards her and covering his head with smooches. "Pretty! Many kisses for you."

Ella regarded the small cut-crystal bottle, half-filled with a bright red liquid, while Tomcat squirmed under Gretel's enthusiastic rain of kisses. "Recruiting?" Ella asked mildly.

"Ah! Ha ha! *Nein, nein*," Gretel protested with a forced laugh, quickly scooping the tiny bottle away out of sight under the counter. She smacked her forehead. "I forget baker man is human."

"Uh-huh," Ella responded.

"Vhat?" Came another voice from somewhere out the back, followed by the appearance of a little blond boy of about twelve years old, peering around a side door. He had a large leather apron over his clothes, a hammer clutched in one hand, and smoked-glass goggles which he pushed up onto his forehead. "Interrupting, alvays interruption! You vant fix vheel today or vhat?"

"*Dummkopf!* Look, is highness," Gretel reproached with a sharp flick of her hand towards Ella.

"Highness Ella!" Hansel responded immediately, setting hammer and task aside he scooted up to the bar, pushed Gretel off the box and clasped his hands over the top of Ella's. His youthful face split wide in a grin, perfect sharp white teeth glinting in the candlelight.

Tomcat sidled up to Ella. Tapped a frantic paw on her shoulder. "These kids have *fangs*," he hissed from the corner of his whiskers.

Ella nodded calmly, trying to convey she was well aware and for him not to be concerned. Or at least, not be overly concerned.

"Vhat!" exclaimed Hansel and Gretel, the siblings exchanging surprised looks. "Your kitty talks!"

Chapter 24

Wake up, Baker!

"Yes, he does talk. Rather too much I have discovered." Ella found herself nodding.

When they had finished laughing, Hansel asked Ella, "How goes the cottage build? I haven't seen Richard—"

Gretel elbowed her brother sharply in the ribs. "*Nein! Dummkopf!*"

Ella pushed out her lips. "It's all right, Gretel." She drew a breath. Exactly how many years had it been since she had last seen Richard? Twenty years, three months and nineteen days...

Hansel smacked his forehead. "Ugh!" He gestured to the near-empty room, waving his hand around as if he searched for the words. "Time..." he said at last with a sorrowful shrug.

Ella could only nod. She caught her elderly reflection in one of the bottles beside the snoring baker. Indeed. Time moved on. No matter how hard one tried to cling on.

Tomcat flinched as Bron jerked and then sat up. The baker wiped the drool from his cheek with the back of his cuff. "Dreamed I was falling," he mumbled to himself.

Gretel nudged Hansel and nodded to the hammer he had set down on the counter.

"*Ja*, ve fix coach vheel," he responded, stepping off the box. "Help yourself," he added to Ella, "Drinks on Simon." —indicating the baker—before following Gretel as she skipped out the side door to the connecting stables.

"Simon was my *grandfather!*" Bron called in irritation after the brother and sister duo and then waved off their disinterested reply of, "Vhatever" with grumbles of, "Live next to someone for forty years, don't even learn your name...

What *are* you looking at?" Bron directed this last statement at Tomcat, perched very close. "Your cat is staring at me!" He rocked back on his barstool, nearly losing balance but Ella steadied him with a hand to his back. "Don't baby me!" Bron snapped. At last fully awake, he groaned on seeing Ella. "Awww, go away, good mother, the bakery is closed."

"So, I guessed." Ella slid off her stool and walked around the back of the bar to investigate the collection of bottles.

"Aye, grab the good whiskey, Hansel keeps it tucked under that shelf there!"

"I think you've had enough to drink," Tomcat voiced.

"I don't think a cat wearing a bow should be telling me what—" Bron started then did a double take. His brows knitted. "Do all cats talk...?"

"No," Ella replied, plonking down a clear bottle, marked *Reviver - Not for Human Consumption*, filled with a noxious-looking thick green liquid, "But the ones that do are very hard to keep quiet."

"Hey!" Tomcat huffed, hunching his shoulders. "I've hardly said anything all day."

"Aye, you tell her, Cat," Bron said, crossing his arms as Ella picked up a shot glass and wiped it clean with a cloth. "I'm not drinking that!" Bron shook his head resolutely, eyes fixed on the vivid green gluggy liquid slowly trickling down the bottleneck as Ella poured a shot.

"What's that smell?" Tomcat said, flicking his tail and covering a paw across his whiskers. "It's like ammonia blended with fermented fish."

"That is Reviver," Ella said with a grin, shaking the last slimy drop free from the lip of the bottle. "Banned over three centuries ago. It gets more potent with age..." She squinted at the green liquid in the shot glass. Tiny bubbles appeared.

"No, no, no!" Bron clamped his mouth shut like a petulant child.

"What's it made from?" Tom enquired, leaning closer to peer into the cup as a curl of vapour rose from within the bubbling green depths. He gagged and moved back.

Ella shrugged. "Dragon urine."

"Eww! You are joking!"

"Mostly."

Bron pushed the glass away and rocked back and forth on his stool. "No, good mother Ella, find another bakery, there's no bread today!"

"What?" Ella demanded, hands on hips. "You think I'm here because I can't get enough of your salted-crust sourdough?"

Bron ceased rocking and cocked an eyebrow. "Yes...? Why else...?"

Ella thumped the steaming odorous cup in front of the baker. "Ginny."

Bron collapsed, crumpled in on himself like a failed soufflé, he sunk forward, forehead to the bar top and wept, "Ginny! My sweet precious, Ginny! What have I done? What have I done?"

Chapter 25

Bron's Tale of the Beginning

"Why don't you start from the beginning," Ella said soothingly, pleased she was, at last, getting somewhere. She fetched up the whiskey Bron had indicated before and poured a double measure in a tumbler.

"Is that a good idea?" Tomcat whispered when Ella slid the drink over to the baker. "He's in bad enough shape as it is."

"The beginning..." Bron uttered, shaking his head. "Where to begin?" Hands clamped about the glass, he stared deep into the amber contents and sighed. "It began when I told Ginny a lie." Bron bowed his head, his chin nearly touching his chest. "A terrible lie."

Tomcat and Ella both leaned closer.

"I told Ginny that I was the Red Unicorn."

"What?" Ella responded, utterly surprised. "But why? Why pretend to be the unicorn? Will Scarlett didn't steal from the rich and give to the poor. He stole from everyone and kept it for himself. He was awful."

"Aye." Bron shrugged. "But Ginny arrived here after Will Scarlett's rebellion. She didn't know him. Hardly anyone knows the true identity of the unicorn, and the more time passes, well, the stories take over the truth."

Ella nodded. "Indeed. Stories get out of control. Rumours twist."

Like the one about a henchman courting the baker's young wife. Anyone who knew how awful Axel was would never think of him and Ginny making a match, but along comes a new man, a kind and handsome man and now, that made an odd kind of logic...

"But why pretend at all?"

"Bah!" Bron snapped as if he'd been asking himself the same thing. "Boredom," he said at last. "The lassie was bored of me." He waved a hand to shush any protest. "Don't say it, yes marriages do have rough patches, but it's the truth... So, I told a tiny, tiny lie and things began to change." A smile appeared on the corner of his mouth. "I told her that I was the Red Unicorn, the outlaw rebel who stole from the rich and gave to the poor."

"And how did you get from that misguided attempt to spice things up to shooting Tom April?"

"What?" Bron's whole body flexed, like a whip cracking. "I didn't shoot Tom April!"

"Really?" Ella demanded. "Was it because you found out Ginny was having an affair with Tom—"

"Hey!" Tomcat cried but Ella held up a finger to silence him.

"—you thought you could put an arrow in him and get away with it because everyone else would blame the unicorn—not Bron the baker!"

"No!" Bron denied it vehemently. "I had nothing against young Tom! It was Axel! Axel who Ginny was cheating on me with!" His face contorted as if something inside had broken. As if this was the first time he'd dared say those words aloud and admit the truth to himself. He slumped. "Yes, I knew... that's why I lied, why I told Ginny I was the unicorn. So she'd find me less boring, more...I don't know. Dangerous. Interesting. And she'd start to love me again."

Tomcat hunched down on the bar counter. Still and quiet for once.

"What I don't understand is," Ella said after a few moments of silence, "how the story you told Ginny got beyond *your* control?"

"Money..." Bron said with a sigh. He swirled the whiskey around and around the tumbler in a golden whirlpool. "Ginny's wee niece and Rum, their business is failing. Do you know how much the stagecoach licence is? Aye, well, Robinne couldn't convince Rum to give it up. A matter of pride, he said. But every month, less business, still the same bills to pay. One day Ginny came to me, said why not take up my red cloak and black arrows again? Rob a few wicked people. Make some money. Save their business."

"Only you couldn't, because you never were the Red Unicorn," Ella comprehended, "and your lie started to unravel."

Bron grimaced. "Aye. She kept nagging at me. Why don't you do this? Why don't you help them?" Bron took a deep gulp of the whiskey. "At last I told her it was because I didn't have my magical black arrows. Without my magical arrows I dared not take up my bow least innocents were hurt."

"I have to give Will credit for that much at least," Ella said. "He was an excellent archer. That's the only part of his story which is true."

Bron looked up. Caught her eye. "Ha! So he had everyone believing. Nay, the black magic arrows were key to his success."

"Wait, what? Are you saying that Will Scarlett actually used *magical* arrows?" Ella was aghast.

Bron grinned. "Oh aye, did you not know that? Did you believe all the nonsense about the unicorn knowing which men were wicked and which innocent? Rubbish. He had magic arrows. Never missed their target."

"I just thought he was a good shot!"

"Aye, he was better than most, that's true. But the black arrows changed everything. Twelve arrows dipped in unicorn blood. That's how he chose his name."

"But using unicorn blood that's more than just magic, that's *black* magic! Black magic is toxic and corrupting, over time it would have poisoned his mind." Ella shook her head in dismay. "I never knew…"

Bron shrugged. "And why should you? Will pulled the wool over everyone's eyes. It's what he was best at."

Ella was reeling. What a terrible mess. From the stables the *dink dink* of a hammer strike intruded on her thoughts and made her wonder, how exactly did Tom fit into all of this?

"Last night," Ella prompted, "what happened with you and Ginny at the Crossroads tavern?"

"Isn't it obvious?" Bron grasped the whiskey bottle and poured himself another tall drink. "Ginny found Will's magic arrows."

CHAPTER 26

THE PRICE AND THE COST

ELLA AND TOMCAT EXCHANGED GLANCES. "Ginny found the black arrows…" Ella repeated, processing this new information. If Ginny found them, how exactly did one end up in Tom? Or the rest of the set with Sibylla?

Bron half-nodded. Closing his eyes, his head bowed low. "Aye," he whispered. "Ginny learned Axel had them."

"What? Axel! How?"

"I don't know, perhaps he confiscated them when Will was finally captured." Bron shrugged as if that detail was unimportant. A tear trickled from the baker's eyes, swiftly followed by more. "Ginny convinced Axel to give her one—she left me a note saying she was going to meet him at the crossroads last night to pay for it—I don't want to think how!" He flung his arms to the bar top and slumped over, sobbing. "It's all my fault—I drove her to it!"

"Oh dear," Ella said, unsure of what else to do or say. Poor Bron, to think such a tiny lie to win his wife's affections back would only drive her into Axel's arms again. That was salt to the wound indeed.

Tomcat signalled her with a tilt of his head to move a little further away. She leaned in close as Tom whispered, "I feel really bad for him. Maybe we should just…you know…leave it be?"

Ella nodded. She'd expected to uncover an evil heart, not a broken one. "Are you sure? We still don't know who shot you or why. If we don't ask now, we might never find out."

"I know, but…look at him…"

Ella regarded the sobbing baker. A full-grown man weeping his eyes out. It was never pleasant to witness pain. And heartache was the deepest kind. Worse than physical wounds, it created a prison of one's own mind. Regret. Blame. She knew all too well.

"You're a kind soul, Tom." She touched Tomcat's paw. "Very well, if this is what you choose, we'll leave it." *For now*, she added silently.

The backdoor opened suddenly; and Gretel peered around the door, her expression unreadable. "Vhat you do to baker?" Then she caught sight of the bottle of Reviver and rolled her eyes as if having found the answer.

"We can't leave him like this," Tomcat added to Ella. "Do you think you can get him home?"

"*Nein*," muttered Gretel, taking command of the situation, "leave to me." She skipped around the bar and manhandled the weeping baker, draping his arm around her shoulder and with a quick wiggle, shunted him up across her shoulders like a very long sack of potatoes. His fingertips brushed the floorboards.

"Sweet mercy!" Tomcat exclaimed wide-eyed as the tiny girl proceeded to carry Bron to the front door. "You don't see that every day!"

"Wait!" Ella cried, pointing to the entrance. "It's daytime!"

Gretel halted, hand on the doorknob.

"Huh?" Tomcat uttered, bewildered.

"I mean, I just mean that the neighbours, er...they'll gossip!" Ella blustered.

Gretel pivoted. "Oh *ja*..." she said slowly, and then gave Ella a conspiratorial wink as she passed her at the counter. "Vouldn't vant people to see baker in such a state, poor *kinder*." She gave Bron a sort of half-pat-half-slap and then exited out the backdoor that connected to the stables.

"Can't that kid go out in the *sunlight*?" Tomcat hissed and jabbed a frantic paw onto the wood of the ancient bar top. "Are you trying to imply that kid...that kid...is a...?"

"Is a *what*?" Ella demanded. "Say it. Say it out loud."

Tomcat shuddered. He gulped. "I can't."

"Good," Ella said, clearing away the used glasses and placing them on a tray under the counter. "Everyone has secrets. It doesn't make them bad people. A little discretion goes a long way. Don't you agree, *talking* cat?"

Tomcat bristled. "I don't know why you're telling me off. I've hardly said a word all day." He sat there flicking his tail while Ella put the bottles back on their shelves and tidied up.

At last she dusted her hands. "Right, let's make a move. Cross your claws we get home to the cottage before Tinkerbelle nibbles on your pumpkin—"

"Good mother Ella!" boomed a voice from outside, interrupting their conversation, "I know you're in there!"

"Magic preserve, now what?" Ella muttered, heading to the tavern door. Was that Axel shouting?

"Come out now!" shouted the voice again. "Come out, in the name of the queen!"

Chapter 27

A Rock and a Ride Home

"**Don't go out there!**" Tom implored, clutching the back of Ella's skirt. "Axel is the queen's executioner—you said so yourself! What if he's here to convict you of *magic*? You'll be hanged!"

On the threshold, Ella paused. The lad had a point. Not for her sake but for his. She had no magic, she had nothing to hide. "Now would be a very good time to put your amateur dramatics to good use in the cat performance of a lifetime." She looked down at Tom who released her skirt.

He nodded. Mimed stitching his lips.

Not quite the performance she was hoping for.

"Here goes nothing." Ella opened the door out on the porch.

Standing out in the middle of the Southgate square in front of the Huntsman tavern, Axel stood to attention. Behind him was one of the royal carriages, the Charming crest emblazoned on its side for all to see.

Clearly, this was official business.

Axel snapped off a crisp salute. "Are you, good mother Ella?"

Ella sighed and cast a covert glance down at Tomcat who was licking a paw as if it was a new flavour of ice cream.

She turned her attention back to the most pressing problem. "Yes, Axel, you know very well who I am." She crossed her arms and narrowed her eyes at the carriage. Was Sibylla inside watching from behind the gauze curtain? What was the point of this demonstration?

Axel unfurled a small scroll and appeared to study it as if reading it for the first time—more likely stalling for extra time in the hope to draw out a nosey neighbour who hadn't heard his shouting. It was a wonder he hadn't brought a flaming pitchfork.

Ella stood her ground and waited. *Nothing to hide, nothing to fear*, she repeated silently.

If Axel was trying to attract attention then he had chosen a poor place to do it. Southgate, once the main entrance into Charmington, was now more often deserted than not, to the point they usually didn't even bother to open the gate. So few people ventured out into Wyld Enchantment Woods via the gravel road now that the iced-over northern river had superseded it for transportation in and out of the township.

"Right," Axel said, nodding to himself as if just having comprehended the full set of instructions. "Good mother Ella, for services rendered to the crown, you are hereby awarded temporary use of this carriage..." Axel turned and gestured to the carriage as if a tonne of gaudily carved oak covered in purple and gold paint and drawn by two white horses with bells on their harnesses could somehow be missed. The coachman, dressed in palace livery, doffed his tricorn hat. "...in order to see you safely home."

"What?" Ella spluttered, standing upright while feeling she needed to sit down immediately. Goodness gracious, Axel wasn't here to arrest her, he was here to reward her! Why?

Thoughts of the magic mirror popped into her mind. The mirror she had returned to Sibylla. Magic preserve, was Sibylla actually grateful for once?

Then it dawned on Ella. Sibylla was no fool. Her sister wasn't thanking her for returning the mirror. She was making it public that Ella was clearly on the queen's side. If there was a rebellion stirring, this little show of pomp and shouting was really a message to say, 'Oy, rebels, don't trust good mother Ella, she's in the queen's pocket.'

She was between a rock and a ride home.

And her knees hurt. Her back ached and she was tired. She should have taken her walking stick with her this morning, but she'd been too proud. Maybe Sibylla was right. Was she too proud?

Ella scooped up Tomcat. Marched past Axel, nodded to the coachman, yanked the carriage door open and flung herself inside onto the plump velvet cushions, momentarily grateful her raised ire had probably allowed her problematic knees to climb the steps. "Are you going to accompany me home?" Ella asked Axel, whose momentary flicker of surprise was once again covered by smugness.

"No, good mother, that isn't included in my instructio—"

"Huzzah. Much cheering," Ella said, closing the door on him, feeling rather tired and grumpy and every one of her many years. She knocked on the ceiling. "Home, driver, please."

"Right you are, ma'am," came a muffled reply followed by a jingle of harness bells. The carriage lurched forward with the clip-clop of hooves as the two horses set the coach in motion.

Ella settled back on the cushions and Tomcat leapt from her lap to sit opposite, beside a woven willow work picnic basket. "There's a knee rug under here," he said, clawing at a fluffy pink blanket folded neatly under the basket. "This will keep you nice and warm."

"Thank you, Tom," Ella said, reaching out and spreading the soft luxurious fabric across her knees. The fabric was scented with jasmine, which Ella breathed in deeply. Jasmine had been her sister Cinderella's favourite flower. Was that a coincidence…?

"This is very thoughtful of the queen," Tom said, lifting a flap on the basket.

The movement dislodged a golden envelope placed on top of the basket. It fell to the carriage floor and Ella bent over to pick it up. Addressed to her, it contained an invitation to the archery contest.

You will attend? was written in Sibylla's flowing cursive. The question was more a statement of fact Ella surmised from the *'You will'* portion being underlined three times.

"Ooh, there's fresh apple pie and candied walnuts and a flask of something…" Tom said, head down in the basket.

"Apple and cinnamon tea," Ella said with cold certainty. She curled a finger about the door curtain and drew it back to watch the snow-covered evergreens as the coach swayed and bumped gently along the gravel road.

The basket wasn't Sibylla being thoughtful, she was reminding Ella of the price of pride. Ella folded the invite away. That was tomorrow's problem.

"Are you sure?" Tomcat replied distractedly, head down, bum up, as he rummaged around in the picnic hamper. "Let's see, what else, pickles, dates stuffed—"

"Dates stuffed with cream cheese, and a single blueberry muffin cut into quarters," Ella finished. She released the curtain and sat back, smoothing her hands across the soft blanket on her lap.

"How'd you know that?" Tomcat enquired, peering over his shoulder.

"Because I know my sister."

"Are these all your favourite things?"

"No, our sister Cinderella prepared a picnic basket exactly like this on the day she died."

CHAPTER 28

RICHARD AND CINDERELLA'S COTTAGE

"Ohhh... gosh that's... Wait—your sister was Cinderella? *The* Cinderella? That means *you're* one of the ugly stepsisters?"

"What did you say?"

"Nothing! I said nothing." Tomcat squirmed on his seat. "Just...er...I think the lady from the hat shop was right, you shouldn't read that copy of *Cinderella*."

"Now I *have* to read it." Ella took the slim volume the haberdashery twins had loaned her from her pocket and examined the cover. The clock tower in the background picture was striking midnight—or midday—no, there was a full moon in the picture too, it was clearly midnight.

Ella opened the cover and read on the title page: *Based on a true story.*

Exactly how close was this story to what had happened to her sister? And if it was based on her family, who would want to profit from their tragedy?

Ella scanned the title page for the author, but the author accreditation was cryptic: *written by the Sisters Grimm.*

"Grim indeed," Ella muttered under her breath and tucked the book away. She'd read it later. When she wasn't in a bumping, swaying, coach. The motion might induce headaches or nausea after all. "Do you know what I've been wondering?" she asked Tom.

"Is it the difference between turtles and tortoises—that's been bugging me too."

"No, Tom—although I think Merlin might have left an encyclopaedia at home you could read if you really must know. What I've been thinking is, Sibylla wrote your instructions, but when I gave the mirror back, she didn't appear to know it was missing."

"Because it wasn't missing, she thought I had the mirror."

"I suppose."

"I'm glad you got it back safely to her. Why didn't you say the queen is your sister earlier? I wouldn't have worried if you'd told me."

"Wouldn't worry that I might keep the mirror, you mean."

"You did say it was worth a lot several times…"

"Indeed. Don't let that food go to waste," Ella said, drawing her stoic resolve close to her like she might wrap herself in a familiar cloak. Keep your head held high and carry on, that was Ella's motto. "I'll have the dates if you don't care for them."

Tomcat's feline grin returned, and he flipped the cover open on the basket and was quickly rooting around in the treats again.

"So…the thing I'm wondering, with Queen Sibylla being your sister," Tomcat began a few moments later after Ella had helped him open the jar of candied walnuts.

"My twin sister actually," Ella answered, chewing on a stuffed date. She'd forgotten how sweet they were, but the cream cheese was still delicious—and didn't get stuck in her teeth.

"Really, but why do you look so old?"

Ella choked. She thumped her chest and gulped down the date. "You don't shy from questions, do you?"

"Sorry," muttered Tomcat, throwing walnuts up in the air and catching them deftly in his feline jaws, despite the unpredictable bounce of the carriage wheels. He'd certainly kept all Tilly's reflexes. "But is that part of the punishment—you had your wand snapped and were cursed with old age?"

Ella thought about reminding him of the proverb, *curiosity killed the cat.*

"The wand breaking didn't curse me with age, it released the years that had been held back in one big hit," Ella responded, setting the dates aside and peering into the picnic hamper. The apple pie smelled wonderful. Apple pie had been Richard's favourite.

"But wait, so Queen Sibylla is really as old as you…?"

Ella helped herself to the muffin instead, and sat back, leaning into the cushions. "We were born minutes apart. And before you ask, I'm two hundred and thirty-three years old."

"What!" Tomcat sprayed a mouthful of half-chewed walnuts and started coughing. "I mean, you look very good then, for your age," he added once he caught his breath again.

"Thank you so very much," Ella replied tight-lipped.

"But why would Sibylla ban magic if she's the same as you?"

"My sister never managed to earn a wand." Ella shrugged. "Long story short. If she can't use magic, she decided no one else can either."

"That's not very fair."

"Who said life was fair?" Ella picked the blueberries off the top of the muffin. They were sourer than she remembered. Was nothing as it had been?

"But if Queen Sibylla is as old as you *and* she doesn't have a wand, why does she still look young?"

"Wyld magic preserves youth and Sibylla was born with wyld magic, she just can't control it." Ella gestured outside to the snow-covered trees. "This eternal winter is her doing though it's unintentional." Memories of childhood flooded back. Of ice-skating with their beloved mother. "Sibylla loved winter as a child. In the schoolroom she struggled, but on the ice, she outdid us all... She had no rival for speed or grace..." Ella gave herself a mental shake. "Goodness, listen to me harp on like an old woman. Are you going to pick up those nuts you dropped everywhere, or do I have to chide you like your mother?"

Tomcat's ears dipped and Ella regretted her poor choice of words. The lad was an orphan after all. "I'll do it," she blustered, picking up the half-chewed fragments, "your little thumbless paws aren't suited for it anyway."

Tomcat held his paws in front of his face like he needed the reminder he was wearing another's shape. "Have you ever been in love?"

"That's an odd question." Ella swept the walnuts briskly from the cushions into her palm. Goodness, Tomcat was shedding white hair too. It was sticking to the velvet. Whose idea was it to have velvet cushions in a coach? Really! Didn't Sibylla have anything better to spend her money on than ridiculous cushions?

"I was just thinking..." Tomcat sighed. "What if I'm stuck as a cat forever!"

"Come on now, you've only been a cat for a day, not even a full day."

"But have you? Been in love?"

Ella closed her eyes. "Once."

"What was his name?"

"Richard. He was a woodcutter. Humble but hard-working, and smart as a whip." Ella opened her eyes but looked away. Out onto the tranquil trees that Richard loved. Sometimes he used to sing as he walked this path...

'Sing me a song of a lass who'll be queen, say could that lass be mine?'

Ella regarded the crumbs in her hand. "And before you ask, it didn't work out. Richard never loved me back, he was in love with my sister Cinderella."

Tomcat's ear drooped and shoulders hunched. "I'm sorry, that must have been hard on you."

"It was a long time ago. I hardly think of him now." Ella slid the window sash on the carriage door open and scattered the walnut pieces out onto the snow. She peered out the window and looked behind in time to see little sparrows flit down from the trees. "Life goes on, as they say..." Ella breathed in a lungful of crisp mountain air and listened to the clip-clop of the coach horses' hooves and the dainty jingle of their harness bells.

"Can you get your magic back?"

Ella closed the sash and sat back. "My ban ends in thirty years. Perhaps earlier if I'm lucky. Exceptional services to fairy-kind and the Grand Council might restore my wand."

"Thirty years! What kind of exceptional services? Like doing good deeds?" Tomcat's whiskers fanned as he blinked up at her. "Turning men trapped as cats back into men?"

"Wishful thinking I'm afraid." Ella clasped her hands in her lap to warm her chilled fingers. How quickly the cold seeped in. "The Fairy Council doesn't care much for human business unless it generates a lot of goodwill they can capitalise on—like the whole sword in the stone affair my brother Merlin orchestrated."

Tomcat just looked blank.

"You know. Merlin, court magician, everyone knows my name, smug old goat. He had King Arthur pull some sword out of a stone to prove his birthright."

"Never heard of him."

"And yet Cinderella—local girl marries local boy—*that* you've heard of?"

"But she married a prince! A fairy godmother made her a silver dress and a carriage from a pumpkin!"

"What are you talking about? Cinderella *was* a fairy! She made her own dress! She gave up her magic to marry Richard. To live a human life. It was a huge sacrifice."

"That's not how the story goes. She was poor and bullied by her awful sisters and a handsome prince marries her, and she gets to live in a castle!"

Ella rolled her eyes. "Stories! She already lived in a castle, she gave up everything to live with Richard, the poor woodcutter, in his cottage in the woods."

"Cottage..." Tomcat blinked, head tilting, as he fit the pieces together. "...your cottage?"

"Yes, my cottage. Richard built it with my help. I shouldn't have helped but I did." Ella felt old emotions bubbling up, emotions she tried so hard to keep pressed deep down. "I used my magic—not for them, not to help them but for me! I thought if Richard spent enough time with me, he'd see he loved me, not her... It was a stupid, selfish thing and I paid the price."

"So, you risked losing your magic just to try to win the heart of the man you loved, knowing that if he did ever love you back, you'd have to give up your magic to live a human life with him, and in fact you did end up losing your magic...?"

"Yes. I suppose."

"That is so romantic!"

"Nonsense, it was foolish and...and stop looking at me like that! Tom April you are the most soft-hearted fool I have ever met!"

"Aside from yourself, you old romantic you!"

CHAPTER 29

DIRK TURPIN

RIVERSIDE COTTAGE, WYLD ENCHANTMENT WOODS.

Ella was dozing by the time the coach meandered its way along the old road through the forest, to at last pull up beside the ancient silver oak that marked the fork in the road. The main road carried on to the Crossroads tavern, while the minor path, only wide enough to walk down led to Ella's home: Riverside cottage.

The coachman knocked and then opened the carriage door. "Allow me, ma'am," he said, offering his gloved hand to Ella.

Taking hold of his steady arm, Ella looked him over as he helped her down from the coach steps. He was uniformed in a purple frock coat, head topped with a black curled wig and smart black tricorn. Perhaps Tom could try his hand at coaching rather than henching once he recovered?

Once on solid ground, Ella scooped Tomcat into her arms while the coachman fetched the basket. "What's your name, dearie?" Ella enquired. "I will commend your driving to the queen when next I see her."

"Dirk Turpin, ma'am, thank you, ma'am," he replied, and then, looking a little sheepish, pulled a folded newspaper from the deep pocket on his frock coat. "If it pleases you, ma'am, I have finished reading this, perhaps you might like it?"

Ella didn't usually read the *Nottingham Times*. The newspaper was a bit salacious for her taste. She could see '*Werewolves Rampage!*' on the front page, but a covert elbowing in the ribs from Tomcat and Ella found herself happy to accept the offer. Hopefully reading the paper or filling out the crossword would help keep Tom's mind off his pumpkin egg that evening.

Ella nodded and the coachman tucked the paper into the basket of goodies.

"Thank you, Dirk." That was kind. No doubt he thought her a lonely little old lady with nothing to entertain except knitting or pinecone-based arts and crafts.

Dirk offered his arm again after gesturing to the narrow path between the trees from which a thin slice of Ella's upstairs window was just visible in the fading afternoon light.

"Do you like the uniform?" Ella chatted as they walked the snow-covered path.

"Not at first, ma'am, I confess, but truth be told the wig is better than a woolly hat for keeping me head warm and I'd wear the tricorn any day of the week. Makes me feel like a highwayman," he added with a wink.

Ella chuckled and patted his hand.

His grin faded as they reached the break in the trees on the edge of the riverbank. Across the frozen stream Ella's quaint cottage was dwarfed by the tangle of pumpkin vines and large green leaves. Fortunately, the giant pumpkin was shielded by the overgrowth.

"Gracious, ma'am, begging your pardon but what fertiliser do you use on those plants?" Dirk asked, voice tinged with awe.

"Only the best," Ella said with a dark chuckle. "Blood and bone, dearie, fresh blood and bone!"

Dirk gulped.

"It's a secret mind." Ella winked. "Between highwaymen."

His shocked expression fell away, and the grin returned. "Right you are, ma'am, right you are." He set the basket down, doffed his tricorn and turned back to the gap in the trees, calling, "Until tomorrow, ma'am."

"Tomorrow?" Tomcat said quietly once the coachman's footsteps had faded. "What's happening tomorrow?"

Ella sighed and gently put him down. "The envelope on the basket contained an invitation to the archery contest. Non-negotiable for me, I fear. You don't have to come along if you don't want to."

"Are you going to enter?" Tomcat's ears perked up. He leapt out onto the first steppingstone in the iced-over river.

"Wasn't planning on competing, but I'll go and fill my pockets with canapés." Ella pushed the basket out onto the ice and used it to aid her balance as she crossed the river to the small island on which she'd helped build Richard's cottage, now her home.

Her boots squelched on the far bank, and Ella blinked down at fresh grass peeking up through the ground. That was unusual. This ground was usually frozen solid. She couldn't remember the last time she'd seen new growth. Perhaps it had something to do with the extra wyld magic in the pumpkin patch. She looked around to see Tomcat disappear into the curling vines. No doubt checking on the ripening state of his pumpkin egg.

Ella hefted the basket and carried it across the lawn towards the cottage.

"There you are!" cried an angry voice, and a figure wearing a green cloak rose from where they'd been sitting on the porch steps. Ginny— for it was the baker's wife, a longbow clutched in her hand— demanded, "Where is it?"

"Ginny, dear, I didn't see you there," Ella said, managing to keep a level tone of voice despite being momentarily startled. "You quite blended in..." Maybe blending in among the forest greenery had been the point. Ella cast a covert glance about for Tom, but he was hidden within the pumpkin patch somewhere. "Where is what, my dear?"

"Don't give me that confused old woman act," Ginny snapped, stomping down the steps. "The magic arrow, where is it?"

"Ginny, dear, why don't you come inside for a cup of tea, and we'll discuss this rationally."

"No more talking, I am sick of talking." Ginny scythed the air with her free hand. "I need that arrow and Rum says you have it!"

"Surely Rum's finances aren't so bad you would resort to *cheating* to win the archery contest?"

Ginny looked aghast. "Money? You think this is about money? Rum's business can go hang for all I care—I want that arrow to test Bron's lying heart!"

"Oh, Ginny dear, that's just a myth—like most of the stories surrounding the Red Unicorn—no arrow, magic or otherwise, can tell a good heart from a wicked one. Because people aren't ever entirely one thing or another, no one is black or white."

Tears of frustration formed in Ginny's eyes. "I just need to know the truth, if what Axel said is true—I can't take it anymore! The lies, all the lies!" She collapsed, kneeling on the frozen lawn. The longbow slipped from her grasp. "I don't know who to believe."

"Exactly what did Axel say that has upset you so much?" Ella asked gently.

Ginny scrubbed her eyes with the back of her cuff. "He said Bron wasn't the unicorn, he said Bron *betrayed* the Unicorn—aided in her capture."

Ella placed a hand on Ginny's shoulder as the baker's wife knelt there sobbing. "My dear, my dear, I know that must be distressing to hear, but are you certain you can believe Axel? Hasn't Bron been a faithful and steady—wait a second. Did you say, *her? Her* capture?"

Chapter 30

The Unicorn's Secret

Ella gaped down at the wretched baker's wife sobbing in her yard. "The outlaw calling themselves the Red Unicorn was a *woman*?"

Fresh tears streamed from Ginny's amber-coloured eyes. "Not just any woman—my sister, Yara! And Bron handed her over! He betrayed her!"

Ella blinked. Yara? Ginny's sister—Robinne's mother? The Red Unicorn!

"Magic preserve, I didn't see that coming."

Ella gave herself a mental shake. "But Ginny, wait, you know that can't be true. You never met Will, you came here after Will Scarlett was executed. Will was the unicorn—ask Rum if you don't believe me."

"No, you're wrong!" She forcibly pushed Ella's hand away and clambered to her feet. "Axel said Will Scarlett took the blame, Will only claimed to be the unicorn to protect Yara."

"But Yara was a midwife, she brought life into this world, she didn't rob it at arrow point! And why, why would Bron betray Yara like that? Think about what you're saying!"

"Because Bron loved her, and she rejected him!" She marched off across the frozen river without looking back. "He did it out of spite!"

"Where are you going? Ginny dear, come sit inside, just take a minute to think about this!" Ella called despairingly. "Don't do anything hasty you might regret!"

"I'm going to talk to Rum!" Ginny shouted back before disappearing into the trees. "I want the truth!"

Poor lass. To have her heart broken and world turned upside down. It was distressing to see. At least Ginny had left the longbow behind. That should stop her from getting into further trouble.

Another thought occurred. Surely this ruled Ginny completely out of the running as a possible suspect who could have shot Tom.

A rustle behind her alerted Ella to Tom reappearing through the undergrowth.

"How's the pumpkin? Ripe yet?" Ella asked, stooping to pick up the bow. She frowned. Was this the longbow she'd seen Bron with last night? One bow looked much like another. Some were plain. Admittedly this one was quite decoratively carved.

"Still green," Tom answered with a disgruntled flick of his tail. "Is Ginny all right? She sounded distressed. Should we go after her?"

"Man trouble." Ella rested the bow over one shoulder. "Or *men* trouble to be precise."

"That's the longbow Bron had last night," Tom muttered, answering Ella's thought. "See it's got a distinct FTB."

"Lawks. My thoughts precisely."

Tomcat narrowed his eyes. "Oh really? Touch the FTB."

Ella shrugged and touched a point on the top of the bow.

"Lucky guess."

"Let's put the kettle on," Ella said, picking up the basket and climbing up the porch steps. "I'll go feed and water Tinkerbelle, check on the chickens, while you warm your little paws by the fire and read the newspaper. Maybe check out the work-available column. Did you like Dirk's uniform? I think you'd be a good coachman, you're responsible and you like animals."

"Are you trying to distract me? It's not going to work... Although I quite liked his hat, I can't be a coachman, I get terribly coach-sick."

"You had no trouble just now." Ella walked around the veranda to the back door and lifted the latch.

"I think that's because your cat doesn't get motion sick," Tomcat answered trotting along beside, "in case you hadn't noticed my reflexes are also way better than what they were."

"There's a silver lining." Ella hung the longbow on a hook on the back of the door and set the basket down just inside the kitchen. "Can you unpack this for me? I'll go see if the hens have earned their keep and we can have hard-boiled eggs for tea!"

"You don't cook a lot, do you? Leave prepping dinner to me," Tomcat said, snapping off a quick salute. "Your kitchen is in safe paws."

WHEN ELLA RETURNED TO THE snug little kitchen, having exchanged her snow-damp walking boots for soft, dry slippers, she found Tom had been as good as his word. The wood stove fire was crackling, the kettle just starting to steam. A pleasant fragrance of ginger herbal tea like that he'd prepared that morning once more scented the air. Maybe having Tom as a house guest wouldn't be so bad. He had a good work ethic and certainly knew his way around the kitchen.

Ella placed the eggs she'd collected on the bench and then draped her cloak over the drying rack above the stove before joining Tom at the pine table where he was perched, the *Nottingham Times* newspaper spread under him. She scanned the headlines over his shoulder.

> *Werewolves Rampage! A plague of werewolf-infected rats and mice has been swiftly dealt with thanks to the decisive action of our beloved leader, Prince John...*

"Werewolf-infected mice? Utter nonsense. Where do they find these stories?" Ella seated herself across from Tom who looked up and said,

"This is a treat! I usually have to read a used, day-old newspaper—someone has always done the crossword."

"Lawks, what's a crossword?"

Tomcat's little pink mouth fell open. "Grab out that pencil, I'm going to teach you!"

Ella smiled to herself as he pawed through to the back pages, spread the paper flat, smoothing it out across the table and tapped an etching of an irregular grid. "It's a word game. You read this list of clues here, and they suggest a word which has to fit into the grid. The more words you fill in the grid, the easier it gets. Ready to try?"

"All right," Ella replied distractedly, her thoughts returning to the human drama of the day.

Poor Ginny, poor Bron. How did Ginny ever end up having her head turned by Axel of all people? Goodness, the way she'd been acting, was the lass actually in love with that thug? Then again, her sister Yara had fallen for Will Scarlett and he was no better. Perhaps the Spicer girls had a soft spot for bad boys? Goodness, she'd have to keep an eye on young Robinne for her mother's sake, lest the girl ended up with someone equally unsuitable.

"Are you even listening?" Tomcat interrupted her thoughts.

"Yes, of course, just a little deaf in my dotage." Ella cupped a hand to one ear. "Lawks. What did you say, dearie?"

"One across. A large orange vegetable. Seven letters."

"That's easy. Pumpkin. How very topical." Ella wrote the answer into the grid and then set the pencil down. She cast her eyes out the window to the herb patch where the chickens were scratching around. Tendrils of the pumpkin vines were visible among the rosemary and mint, having grown so much in the front garden it was beginning to encroach on the back.

"Good work. Next clue," Tom continued, "One down. The handsomest man in Nottingham. Two words."

"That seems rather subjective." Ella drummed her fingernails on the tabletop. It was true Axel was no slouch in the looks department, and Will Scarlett had been classically handsome—one of the reasons Ella was sure people let him get away with his oafishness.

"I'll just do this one," Tom muttered, pawing up the pencil. "I should probably say any clues that ask who is the most handsome, richest, smartest, etcetera, the answer is always Prince John." Tomcat clamped the pencil between his two front paws and slowly filled in the answer.

"That doesn't sound like what people say of Prince John around here, but I suppose this newspaper wants to keep its licence..."

How exactly could that arrow have been shot into young Tom last night? Bron *knew* his rival for Ginny's affections was Axel, so why shoot another henchman? And if Bron claimed Ginny had gone to fetch the magic arrow from Axel, why hadn't that happened?

And now Ella thought about it, if Axel had taken one of those arrows from the set Sibylla had, why arrange to meet Ginny at the Crossroads tavern? Why not at the castle? Could Ginny have insisted Rum be involved to check if the arrow was authentic?

"I don't think your head is in the game," Tom said, tapping the newspaper. "You've got your deep-thinking face on."

"And what does my deep-thinking face look like, thank you very much?" Ella responded.

Tomcat stuck out his tongue and crossed his eyes.

"Wrong, that's my clue deduction face, carry on, next clue."

"Next clue—oh another easy one. Worn by Nottingham midwives."

"Ah, does that weird bonnet they wear have a name?"

"Sorry, I should have said, it has three letters."

"Hat! Wig. No, bib! Do they wear bibs?"

"It has to fit in with the answer above which is Prince John, it starts with R."

"Rib?"

"I'll just do this one too. Don't worry, you'll get the hang of it soon. The answer is red. Red is worn by midwives. Like the cloak of the midwife you talked to at the Crossroads tavern."

"Marge's cloak had a red lining, who would think of the lining? That's not a fair clue."

"That's because she was off-duty. Their cloaks are reversible. Didn't you know that? They wear the red side out when working so they can go about their business unhindered, so when they have to go beyond the city walls at night they can be recognized by the watchtower from a distance and not mistaken for a curfew breaker."

Ella stood up. "Magic preserve me!"

"What?"

"I just realised why Will Scarlett evaded capture for so long!" Ella slapped her hand to her forehead. She could see it so clearly now. "I'm such an idiot."

"He was a midwife?"

"No! But his wife Yara was! The Red Unicorn wasn't one person—it was two! Will and his wife Yara—Yara the midwife. The red cloak wasn't to identify him, it was a decoy! Yara drew off anyone in pursuit of Will!"

Chapter 31

Getting Schooled

Tomcat put the pencil aside. "Can I ask you something a little personal?"

"Why stop now?" Ella paced around the room, her mind in turmoil. "My goodness, why didn't I see it before? Maybe Axel's story has some truth in it. Someone must have betrayed him—*them*. The Red Unicorn evaded Sibylla for so long. And then all of a sudden. Captured. Hanged. End of story."

"If you knew Will Scarlett was this outlaw, who from your account was actually a pretty horrible person, and created a lot of trouble for Queen Sibylla, your sister..." Tomcat let the rest of the question hang.

Ella quit pacing. It was a fair question. "Sibylla and I had a bad falling out years before Will started his antics. She wouldn't even speak to me."

"Over Cinderella's death?"

Ella shook her head. "No, that was just the icing on the cake as far as Sibylla was concerned. And truth be told I only suspected Will was the Unicorn. It wasn't until he was caught that my suspicions seemed confirmed. Will was so awful. Arrogant, selfish, foolhardy. If there was a shortcut, Will would take it. I never understood what Yara saw in him."

"What was Yara like?"

"She was lovely. Thoughtful, hard-working. She never had a bad word to say about anyone."

"Intelligent?"

"Very. She wasn't born here, but she could name every bird in the forest by sight or song." Ella studied Tomcat's thoughtful expression. "What are you thinking?"

"Maybe Will wasn't as bad as you thought, or maybe Yara wasn't as nice. What's more likely?"

Ella blinked. Shocked to think that young Tom might have more insight into people she thought she knew.

He carried on, "Sometimes what we believe is due to perspective.

Two days ago I thought witches and magic were awful. Now I know better. Magic is dangerous, but the danger is a side effect. It doesn't force people to behave badly."

Ella sat down. Barely able to speak. "Lawks."

"I'm sorry, I didn't mean to offend you." Tomcat hunched down, crouching on top of the newspaper.

Ella shook her head. "Don't fret, you didn't offend me, just..." She clasped her hands on the tabletop and studied the neat little grid of the crossword.

Life wasn't so tidy. Not everything could be put into little boxes and ticked off. Hearts least of all.

"It's just that it has been a long time since I've been *schooled*. But I'm not so proud that I can't admit, one is never too old to learn." She nodded at him, sitting there with his neat little candy-striped scarf, looking very tense and worried. "Now, how about with your guidance we try to make dinner using the herbs Arabella has sent. You're the chef, consider me your pupil."

THE WIND PICKED UP IN the late evening as Ella and Tomcat sat in her parlour after dinner. The cluckoo clock ticked softly on the mantel. Tomcat poured over the encyclopaedia *The Guide to Creatures of Wyld Kingdom,* which her brother Merlin had written. Every now and then sharing a fact he found interesting with Ella who was reading—or more accurately, pretending to read the copy of *Cinderella*—while in her mind she played over the events of the day. The elusive question: *who shot Tom April and why?* foremost on her thoughts, a nagging hindrance like a seed stuck in a tooth.

Robbery? Grudge? Mistaken identity? What else? What clue was she missing?

When she finally went upstairs to her attic bedroom, she sat up in bed for a long time, staring out the window, listening to the surrounding fir trees sway in the wind. The cottage creaked and groaned all night till at last the wind dropped and Ella's mind settled enough to allow her rest, until...

"Tom!" Ella bellowed, sitting bolt upright in bed. "Tom, the arrow! The arrow!"

"What? What is it?" came the muffled urgent cry from below followed by the bang of a chair toppling over.

Ella shunted aside the feather quilt and wiggled from the soft mattress. Dragging on her dressing gown while groping for the handrail in the faint pre-dawn light she hobbled downstairs.

She found Tomcat peering out the front parlour window, shouting out to any would-be villain lurking in the pumpkins, "I'm armed! I've got a poker!" He looked over his little furry shoulder as Ella entered. "Is the killer back? What did you see?"

"No," Ella replied, buttoning up her robe. "Where's the black arrow? I need to look at it."

Tomcat pointed to the sideboard where all his worldly possessions extracted from his pockets had been collected. "Why? What is it?"

In the gloomy light, Ella fetched up the black arrow and took it over to the window to aid her eyesight. She squinted. "Look this over for me, my eyes aren't good enough in low light, look for a maker's mark." She placed it on the windowsill in front of Tomcat.

"What are you expecting to find?" he muttered, examining the arrow shaft and fletchings closely.

"Something Ginny said last night—it jolted me from sleep. She said Rum told her I had the arrow—but I didn't tell Rum that! I only asked Rum if he knew who made black arrows. The only other person that knew we had this arrow was Bron! Not Rum. Don't you see what that means?"

Tomcat's hackles stood up. "Rum shot me?"

Ella nodded. "Most probably."

"What?" Tom nearly spat. "But, but why? What did I do to him? I never even met him until yesterday."

"I know, I know," Ella said, trying to soothe his justified indignation. "Most likely you were simply at the wrong place at the wrong time."

Tomcat shook himself, his fur spiky with outrage. "What's all this got to do with a maker's mark?" He placed a paw on the arrow. "Not that I can find one. It does smell unpleasant, that's all I can tell."

"Because Rum makes and sells magical things—he told us Axel brings him things to sell. What if Axel needed Rum to make a replacement for an arrow he stole from the queen's set so he could sell the original arrow to Ginny?"

"What?" Tomcat's tail flicked. "Queen Sibylla has more of these arrows? A whole set? When were you planning on telling me that?" He held up a paw, cutting off her answer. "Even if what you're suggesting is true, why does it even matter who made the arrow?"

"Because if it's a genuine magical arrow, and not just a fake that Axel painted black to fool Ginny, then it proves Rum was involved."

Tomcat frowned. "I'm not sure it does."

Ella placed her hands on her hips. "It made sense to me when I was half asleep. Let's at least test this arrow, find out if it's magic." She grabbed the arrow and headed for the kitchen where she'd hung the longbow Ginny had left behind on the coat hook on the back door.

"And if it is?" Tomcat asked, falling into step behind her.

Ella paused on the threshold, to thrust her bare feet into her boots. "Then we *win* the grand archery contest."

"What?"

"After we confront Rum, naturally."

CHAPTER 32

TESTING THE ARROW

"You are joking? You wouldn't really cheat?"

"Of course not! Goodness, it's nippy." Ella's breath puffed white clouds as the outside chill hit her lungs. Tomcat huddled on the shelter of the veranda while Ella walked down the back porch steps, the longbow in one hand, the arrow in the other.

"Looks like it might snow," Tom muttered.

Ella cast her gaze up. The lad was right. The light had that slightly odd glow. If it did, fresh snow would make walking to the Crossroads tavern a struggle. The sooner they had this done the better.

Ella looked left and right, searching around for a suitable target to test the arrow. The pumpkins in the front garden were an obvious choice, but she didn't want to risk upsetting Tom. Not to mention, there was something unsettling about aiming for a living target. Even though it was a plant, there was no denying the pumpkins had personality.

The moment she set foot into the frosty backyard, the tendrils of plants started to sway and rustle as if wondering what she was up to.

Curious pumpkins and a talking cat. Could things get any stranger?

"I guess the horseshoe nailed to the door of Tinkerbelle's stable will make do for the target," Ella said to herself. The target itself wasn't important, nothing elaborate was required.

"When did you last use a bow?" Tom asked as she nocked the arrow to the string.

"I'm not going to lie, it's been a while," Ella said, drawing back, taking the strain on her arms as the longbow flexed, and aiming the arrow tip to her prescribed horseshoe target twenty feet away. "Quit the chat, I need to concentrate..."

The horseshoe...the horseshoe...centre of the horseshoe...

—Zzzing—

The arrow hissed through the air and *thwacked* into the door of the donkey shed, precisely dead centre of the horseshoe. It was exactly as her sister Sibylla had said, the arrow hit the target where she'd aimed. Ella grinned. "Ta-dah!"

"That wasn't very magical," Tom said, spoiling her flush of success. "I think even Tinkerbelle could have hit that."

"Oh really!" Ella replied, a bit miffed. She strode over to the stable and wriggled the arrow shaft free from the wooden planks. "What do you suggest then? How do we prove the arrow is magic? Arrows either hit the target or not. There's no fireworks built-in, you know!"

Tomcat tugged at the candy-striped scarf wrapped around his neck. "How about we make this...interesting?"

"A blindfold!" Ella protested. "You are joking!"

But a few moments later Ella stood out in her back garden, the soft warm cloth of Tom's scarf bound over her eyes, and the arrow tip wavering towards the front of the shed where she'd seen the horseshoe only seconds before.

"One more thing," Tomcat called out. "Turn around three times!"

"You cannot be serious!" Ella said. "Are you testing the arrow or my dignity?"

"I'll hide behind a porch post," Tomcat called, "don't worry, I'll be perfectly safe."

"I wasn't worried about you, but I don't want to have to replace a window!"

"Come on, three times now," Tomcat called encouragingly. "Don't be a fraidy cat!"

"Very funny," Ella muttered, shuffling around. Goodness, that was surprisingly disorienting! After just the first turn she had no idea which direction she was pointing. All senses were limited to the sound of her breathing and her footsteps as she moved.

Once, twice... Magic preserve. This was crazy!

Ella drew back and took the strain. Goodness, without her sight she couldn't even tell if she'd drawn the bow back enough.

The horseshoe...centre of the horseshoe... Maybe she should just pull back on the bow a little more? The horseshoe... Had she turned three times, or was it only two? Maybe she should move around a bit more.

And then she tripped.

—Zzzing—

CHAPTER 33

LONG LIVE THE REVOLUTION!

"HORSESHOE!" Ella shrieked then hit the ground hard.

The wind knocked from her lungs. The bow dug painfully into her ribs. She yanked the scarf off her eyes. Magic preserve, she'd shot at her house! "Tom, speak to me, are you all right?"

Tomcat peeped out from behind the porch post.

Ella let her breath out. Sagged on the cold ground. "Thank the stars! You're alive!"

"Aww, you big softie." Tomcat padded up to her, then sat there preening. "You will miss me when I leave, won't you?"

Ignoring him, Ella pushed up from the ground. "What did I hit? Anything?"

"See for yourself." Tom pointed in the other direction across to the stables where the arrow was vibrating, once more lodged in the centre of the horseshoe. "Now that's a ta-dah!"

Ella was less thrilled. "I was really hoping this arrow was a fake," she admitted after prying it out of the stable door. She lifted the latch and peered inside. Tinkerbelle was asleep and snoring in her stall. Not disturbed by the noise they had made. Good.

"But why?" Tom asked. "What does it matter if the arrow is magic or not?"

Ella closed the barn door gently and turned to Tom. "Because it proves whoever shot this arrow was purposely targeting you."

Tomcat's ears flattened. "I guess so. I can't imagine why."

"Neither can I," Ella responded. "Let's go ask."

"Ask who? Rum?"

Ellen nodded, heading back inside the cottage to get dressed.

Tomcat fell in step behind her and tugged at the hem of her dressing gown. "No, I don't think you should. It's too dangerous." He sat at the foot of the stairs as she climbed up to her attic bedroom. "What if he tries to hurt you? I'm too small to stop him!"

"He can't kill me, I'm immortal."

"Really?" said Tom, eyes wide with wonder.

"No, not really," Ella said, closing the bedroom door.

"This is no time for joking!" Tom called. He carried on muttering and complaining and trying to get her to change her mind while she dressed. "We should go tell the queen. I work for her, and you're her sister."

Don't keep reminding me, Ella thought, exchanging her nightgown for her Sunday best. Ella's finger poked through a hole in the side seam of her bodice. Oh, well, no one would see under the cloak anyways.

"The queen will help us," Tom added, "she'll know what to do."

"There's a first time for everything," Ella muttered as she buttoned up the outfit. Somehow she doubted that day was today.

Last on, her scarf and gloves. Ella paused to study her aged reflection in the oval dressing table mirror. Opening the top left-hand drawer, she felt around the collection of lace handkerchiefs until her questing fingers found what she sought. A small silver locket, the outer decorated with two unicorns. Inside a miniature painting of Richard. Her sister Cinderella had commissioned this portrait for Richard's twenty-first birthday. His fair hair, green eyes and charming smile were captured for eternity.

How long now since she had seen those emerald-bright eyes, that smile? How many years since Richard disappeared?

Ella thought about taking the locket with her for good luck but dismissed the notion as foolish. The sentimental thoughts of a sad old woman. Ella Charming was neither.

Admittedly she was quite elderly but that was a technicality. And age might not have given her wisdom, but it certainly had dished out experience. She knew exactly what to do.

"I'm not going to rush off accusing Rum of anything, I have no intention of putting myself or you—or anyone in danger," Ella told her fretful house guest when she descended from the attic.

"That's a relief."

"No, I'm going to join his rebellion."

"What?" demanded Tomcat, aghast. "You're going to do what?"

Ella rifled through the slippers beside the umbrella stand. "Where is my other boot? Did I leave it by the fire?" Ella shuffled into the kitchen, but the missing walking boot wasn't propped up by the wood stove to dry. Hands on hips she turned to Tomcat. "Did you hide my boot?"

Tomcat clasped his paws and looked away, his telltale eyes flicking towards the pantry. "No."

With a sigh, Ella hobbled into the dimly lit pantry. *Where had that troublesome cat—*

"Aha!" Tomcat shouted triumphantly, slamming the pantry door closed and trapping her inside.

"Very clever."

"Too right! It's for your own good," Tom voiced from the other side of the door. "You may not care what happens to you, but I do!"

Ella's irritation was only momentary. She placed her palm on the pantry door. Tom meant well. He cared.

It was an odd feeling. This youthful stranger, who should be charging off to the tavern right now, ready to confront his attacker, was instead putting her well-being before any desire for revenge. What had happened to the youth of today? They were...surprising.

"You're unnaturally quiet," Tomcat said.

"Ohh, I'm the chatty one!" Ella was about to launch into a tirade when a thought occurred. "Are you trying to distract me?"

"I learned from the best."

Ella smiled.

CHAPTER 34

THE PLAN GOES AWRY

THE OLD ROAD, WYLD ENCHANTMENT WOODS.

"So, what's the plan?" Tom enquired as he and Ella, longbow in hand as an impromptu walking stick, trudged along the old road that wound its way through the tall fir trees of Wyld Enchantment Woods.

Robbery. Grudge. Mistaken identity.

These three notions repeated through Ella's thoughts as she walked towards the Crossroads tavern.

She'd been looking at it all wrong from the start. She'd dismissed the idea that Tom had put forth of Sibylla's concern that there was a new rebellion afoot. Rebellions were born from grudges. It didn't matter that Tom himself had done nothing to cause the grudge, he was an unwitting symptom of a bigger disease.

Perhaps Sibylla was right. Surely it was pride that had her ignore Sibylla's worry. That and the fact—or rather the assumption—that she knew her neighbours. Maybe she did. But did she know their breaking point?

Rum had personally been greatly affected by Sibylla's ban on magic. He was a master craftsman prevented from openly plying his trade—for years forced underground. Bullied. Ground down under Axel's boot. And now he couldn't even afford to keep the stagecoach licence—another problem that could be squarely placed at Sibylla's feet—this eternal winter was her doing.

The winter had lasted so long that all the rivers had iced over, and while it had made fortunes for enterprising types realising how much quicker and easier it would be to transport goods and people via a smooth 'ice road' rather than the muddied old gravel road, deeply rutted and frequently hampered by fallen trees, it had sunk as many fortunes.

Both sources of Rum's income had been depleted all due to Sibylla. Why wouldn't he start to warm to the idea of rebellion? He had the resources, he knew the people, he knew the area. Possibly he'd overheard Ginny mentioning the legend of Will Scarlett and an idea had started to seed in his mind. What if he led his own rebellion, unlike Will's it wouldn't be just to line his pockets, of course not, it would be to restore the thing that Charmington had once valued, had prided itself on—magic.

"Sorry, what did you say?" Ella muttered as she was forced to go around another fallen tree. Goodness! It was no wonder that Hansel and Gretel's stagecoach had broken a wheel. This road was clearly not being maintained at all. She would have taken her usual shortcut through the forest if not for Tom pestering her to at least stay visible on the main road. So-called main road—it was becoming an impassable track with each new day.

"The plan," Tomcat replied, leaping over the fallen log and waiting on the other side while Ella took the long way around. "I only let you out of the pantry because you swore you had a sensible plan."

"Yes, the plan, of course. We go in, buy a drink, maybe a round for whoever is there, start complaining about the queen. Once I have them onside, I'll mention I found a dead henchman—you—and I'll loudly praise whoever took out one of Sibylla's worthless lackeys."

"No one's going to believe that!" grumbled Tom as they trekked along, his little paws making round dents in the snow. "You're her sister!"

"Forgive me for rubbing it in, but you have no experience in sibling relationships, so trust me. They will entirely believe me because I'll be speaking from the heart. Those that don't know Sibylla and I are twins—and there are many—we don't exactly look alike, and she's barely acknowledged me for the past two decades. Well, they have their own grudges against our beloved ruler. You weren't here when she banned magic. It was a dark time. Businesses forced to close. Good people run out of town."

"But I heard Rum himself say this morning that no one who remembered the dark days would go against her—I thought he meant she restored the peace."

"That is a matter for debate! So, like I was saying, we get people venting their frustrations and just you mark my words, before we leave Rum will come and have a quiet word. If he is the head of this rebellion—and who better?—he'll welcome me with open arms. I'll have his confession of your demise before noon!"

"But this is all just pretend? You wouldn't really betray your sister?"

Ella bit her lip. Would she? That was the question. If push came to shove, if snap came to crackle, would she pop?

"Do you smell something?" Tomcat said, standing on his hind legs and sniffing the air.

"Smoke!" Ella pointed as they rounded a bend in the road and came out from the shrouding trees. The view opened up to reveal the small valley below where the gravel road from Charmington crossed paths with the main road to Nottingham and the back roads up to the gold-rich mountains. A dark column of billowing smoke roiled higher than the trees.

There was only one place it could be coming from.

"Magic preserve, the tavern is on fire!" Ella started to run, her hobnail thick-soled boots jarring her with each step, but despite the pain, she ran toward the smoke. People were in danger!

Tomcat zoomed off ahead, a flash of white fur against the white snow, his little feet pock-marking the road like a trail of breadcrumbs straight to disaster.

THE FIRE WAS IN THE ROOF, or so it appeared to Ella when she made it down to the tavern clearing. A chain of people shovelled buckets of snow into the building while others carried out items of furniture. Tables and chairs, pots and pans, all stacked higgledy-piggledy out in the snow. All this snow and ice and yet so little water!

Robinne manned the water pump in the backyard, her face set with grim determination. Ginny was weeping, an inconsolable lump, shrieking and wailing as neighbours, gold miners and pedlars came to the tavern's aid.

Ella stumbled up to Robinne, discarded the longbow and clamped onto the pump handle. "I can't carry buckets, but I can pump!" she said near breathless from running.

"That's my bow!" Robinne said, brows knitted. Shaking herself as if now wasn't the time, she rushed off with the precious water, and another person thrust a bucket under the pipe as Ella yanked down. Water splashed everywhere but the pedlar didn't even step back, instead letting the water slosh his boots. No time for finesse. Keep pumping, keep pumping!

"Pull yourself together!" Ella shouted at Ginny. "Possessions can be replaced!"

The baker's wife only pointed at the roof, big gulping sobs racking her body. "Rum!" she wailed, pointing to the thick black clouds pouring from the rafters. "Please! Axel and Rum are still in there!"

"Good gracious what?" Ella baulked, still pumping as two gold miners thrust a tin bath under the pump to collect the water. "Rum is in the tavern?"

"Yes!" wailed Ginny, pointing, begging, "Upstairs—Rum—he, Axel—me—we were fighting! I knocked over a candle! It's all my fault!"

Ella gasped, looking around at the busy hive of people all working together as Robinne returned with her bucket.

The panicked shriek of a horse tethered to the hitching post nearby made Ella's stomach drop.

Where for that matter was Tom? Ella suddenly realised she had lost sight of him. Would he have been foolish enough to go inside?

A loud crash made her flinch. Glass sprayed out from the upstairs windows and then somebody wrapped in a red cloak jumped from a window out onto the porch roof.

Magic preserve, it was Axel! Wait! And Tomcat too!

"Tom!" Ella shouted as the white cat and Axel ducked as a *boom!* rang out from the tavern and a wave of red and purple flames roiled above all their heads and disappeared.

Purple flames. That did not bode well. Unicorn blood burned purple. Had Rum been messing with black magic?

Face and clothing blackened with soot, but otherwise appearing unharmed, Axel climbed down from the porch roof. Ginny ran up to him, but Ella didn't catch their words as she instead ran to gather up Tomcat who had likewise dropped to the ground and was coughing uncontrollably. "Where's Rum?"

"Rum is dead," Axel muttered, thinking Ella had spoken to him, "I would be too if it wasn't for that cat." He wrenched off the red cloak and shoved it into Ginny's arms, muttering, "Yours, I believe." And without looking back, stomped past them both and unhitched his frightened horse from the post.

Magic preserve, had Axel actually been a member of their rebellion?

"Keep going, it's nearly out!" a voice shouted from the bucket chain, rousing the others to redouble their efforts.

Ella carried Tom to the edge of the fir trees and scooped up snow, letting it melt in her palm. "Lick this, it will help soothe the smoke in your lungs." Tom nodded and did as bid. His lovely—Tilly's lovely—white fur was all gritted and grey with soot. Magic preserve! Foolish boy, he could have died! "Are you hurt?"

Tomcat shook his head. Covering his feline mouth with his paws he coughed again. "Smoke," he rasped, "just the smoke."

Only then did Ella become aware that Robinne and Ginny were shouting at each other.

"Everything he worked for!"

"All our stores!"

Were they blaming or consoling? Ella couldn't tell. They were also cradling each other and weeping.

"Is it true?" Ella asked Tom. "Rum is dead? What happened?"

Tomcat nodded, coughed some more and then rasped, "Rum fell from the loft balcony into the common room below."

"Did you see him fall?"

"He was on the ground when I got there. Took his pulse." Tomcat paused to draw breath as if he couldn't suck enough oxygen into his small frame. His chest heaved. "Dead—spine snapped maybe—clipped a table. Instant. Must have been instant." His body contorted as another bout of coughing spasmed through him.

"I'm taking you home," Ella said, getting to her feet. "Once I know you're well I will see what I can do for Ginny and Robinne."

A family had been torn apart, but she had Tomcat to take care of first.

Chapter 35

Quick, Call the Hairdresser

"**Why are you annoyed?**" Tomcat asked from the crook of Ella's left arm as she strode the old road homewards, her right arm occupied with jabbing a tree branch she was using as a walking stick into the frozen ground with each step.

"What makes you think I am annoyed?" Ella responded, increasing her pace as she neared the familiar landscape of Riverside cottage.

He peered up at her. "Your face is all scrunchy..."

"Walking through this snow is harder than it looks—perhaps you may understand when you're in your third century. As for my face, once again you have misinterpreted my furrowed brow for deep thinking. I have come to the conclusion that despite your protests this morning it was in fact you, not I, that put us in danger—or to be precise you put Tilly in danger."

"Gosh, Ella, I'm sorry. I didn't think of it like that, but you're right of course. You're right to be annoyed at me."

"I feel that having known me for precisely two days you are in no way shape or form in any position to be judging my internal mechanisms. I am a rather elderly lady, we are known for rambling, lawks, indeed.

In fact, I was merely contemplating, one, how much time and hot water it's going to take to get Tilly's fur back to its pristine condition when what I really need is a long sit down. And two, that despite our best efforts we are even further from finding out who might have shot you, assuming the truth has died with Rum. Three, despite your foolish propensity for being spontaneous, not ever knowing your place, never holding your tongue or acting in a calm and rational manner, that I am rather proud of you.

And perhaps I might even commend you on your bravery. You saved a man's life today, that is a noble deed, even though the man himself has so far displayed actions that might only be described as not noble, or un-noble if that's a word."

"Was that a compliment?"

"No, merely an observation of fact."

"I observed a fact today too. Rum can't have shot me."

"What?" questioned Ella, coming to a stop underneath the giant silver oak that marked the fork in the path to her cottage.

"When I took his pulse," Tomcat explained as Ella set him down, "I saw bruising several days old. I think his arm was much worse than he was letting on yesterday, possibly even broken."

"So, he couldn't have drawn a bow to shoot you..." Ella reached the same conclusion that Tom must have. A jingle of bells made her look about.

"Ma'am, good morning!" called the coachman they had met yesterday, Dirk Turpin, doffing his tricorn as the coach appeared around a bend. "I'm here to fetch you for the archery contest."

Oh, that. She'd forgotten about the invitation. Why exactly did Sibylla even want her to attend?

"Thank you, Dirk, I'll just be a moment, I forgot to put on my good cloak."

"I thought that was your good cloak?" whispered Tom at her feet as she headed for the riverbank.

"It is, I'm stalling to let you go inside, you can warm up, maybe have a wash. I'll be back as soon as I can."

"I'll come with you," Tom said, "I don't want to leave you on your own and I feel fine now other than a raspy throat."

"Only if you're sure you're up to it," Ella said, secretly grateful for the company. She had asked for a long sit down—it seemed she was about to get it.

"No need to change the cloak, ma'am," Dirk called back, and drawing in the reins, he knocked on the coach roof. "Goldilocks is waiting inside; she has everything you'll need—queen's orders. Not that you need it, you look perfectly nice as always."

"Goldilocks?" Tomcat whispered as the coachman leapt down.

"Sibylla's hairdresser," Ella murmured. A thought occurred and she walked over to Dirk. "How is Goldilocks with cats? Mine is quite grimy this morning."

"Oh goodness, so he is, wouldn't recognise him for being the same cat as yesterday," Dirk responded, and he offered out his arm for Ella. "Why, he's more grey than white. Like he aged a hundred years overnight."

Can happen to the best of us, Ella added silently as the carriage window slid open and Goldilocks herself leaned out, a comb in one hand and a spray bottle in the other.

"Are you ready for the royal treatment?" Goldilocks said, her voice high-pitched with glee, as she welcomed Ella inside.

Once Ella was settled in, Goldilocks took care of Tomcat, merely clucking her tongue at the dirty condition of his coat before wiping down his sooty fur with a hot, wet towel and applying various floral scented lotions.

"Oops, nearly forgot," Goldilocks chatted as the coach swayed and bumped along the path toward Charmington. She nodded to a golden envelope protruding from a pocket on the side door. "Instructions from our beloved ruler."

Ella took the offered envelope but tucked it in her skirt pocket instead of reading it as it was rather cramped in the carriage this morning with all Goldilocks accoutrements of trade plus several items of clothing. Goldilocks herself took up no space at all, she was like Rum, one of the small people, a true craftsman. Only her trade was now fashioning hairstyles.

"Here, take your cloak off, Sibylla wanted you to wear this," Goldilocks told Ella while wrapping Tomcat in a clean, dry towel, she somehow managed to keep drying his fur while helping Ella into a rather gorgeous garment that was a cross between a cloak and a coat. "It's called a coat-dress," Goldilocks said, hairpins in her mouth, she strapped a wide gold belt around Ella and cinched it in, giving her a tiny waist in comparison to the volume of purple fabric flaring out.

Tomcat was unusually silent, perhaps due to his sore throat, or having learned his lessons at last, or just relaxing under the towel treatments, at any rate, he appeared to be quite happy with all the pampering. It was a novelty for him, Ella supposed, and she wouldn't begrudge him that. When did a poor orphan boy get to enjoy luxury usually reserved for the queen? And he had been brave today. He deserved a reward.

"It's not my place to pry," Goldilocks was saying, drawing Ella from her thoughts, and while they travelled, primping and curling Ella's grey hair into a sculptural bouffant. "But you were looking a little worse for wear this morning...?"

"There was a fire at the Crossroads tavern," Ella explained, and told the hairdresser a pared-down version of events, omitting Rum's death, unable to remember if Goldilocks had a direct connection to Rum.

It probably wasn't her place to be the bearer of such bad news.

Clearly, Goldilocks had heard of Rum's financial problems because she launched into listing all the businesses she'd advised him to take over when the queen had banned magic.

"I've been telling Rum for ages, he should have taken over the cluckoo shop—who better? Or the glovers. Now there's a business that won't go out of business while winter lasts! But no, some people won't listen. You've got to move with the times I told him, so what if magic is out? Do you see me complaining?"

Ella let Goldilocks words wash over her, nodding where she thought appropriate and holding a comb or pin as Goldilocks worked her own brand of magic, turning Tomcat into a prize specimen, a fluffy bundle of glossy white fur, with a large purple silk bow, and golden painted claws. Ella had her fingernails done too, and despite all the silliness of it, it gave her time to just sit and be pampered, and not have to think too much about the last few days.

At least the worst must be over.

CHAPTER 36

ARCHERY CONTEST – PART ONE

CHARMINGTON CASTLE.

On arriving at the castle, Ella was escorted from the carriage up to the library where Sibylla was surrounded by the Charmington elite. From the doddering old mayor to elegant ladies of old families, and several well-dressed men that Ella felt she probably should know but couldn't place.

The queen, like the men, was adorned in a fur cloak while the other ladies wore fashionable coat dresses as if they were all about to head back out into the cold at any moment. And assuming they were all gathered to watch the archery contest, they must be.

"My dear," Sibylla drawled, beckoning her over, "don't you look stylish, and you've brought along your cat, how…quaint." Pulling her close, as if to give her a warm embrace, Sibylla hissed in Ella's ear, "Promise nothing but keep him negotiating!" And then, turning towards a blond man of medium height, about thirty, dressed in a black bearskin cloak with a large gold chain, announced, "Allow me to introduce my er, close family member, Granny, I mean, Lady Ella Charming… Prince John, Regent of Sherwood."

Negotiating? Negotiating what? Maybe she should have read those instructions. *Too late now.*

"Lady Ella Charming, charmed, I'm sure. No pun intended," the prince said, clicking his heels, bowing and clasping Ella's cat-free hand in both of his. He planted a big sloppy kiss on her knuckles.

Ella wasn't sure which was worse. The kiss or being called Granny. Nope, it was the kiss. Definitely the kiss.

"When were you last in Wyld kingdom?" Ella asked, patting Tomcat's head distractedly and willing herself not to wipe the kiss slobber off on the side of her new coat.

She took a moment to study the unfamiliar young prince before her, to compare if there was anything about John that reminded her of Tom. If not for what Tom had said, the thought wouldn't even have crossed her mind. She could see little resemblance. Admittedly there was something familiar about John, but in an unsettling way, like a childhood teddy bear with the face pushed in and eyes ripped off. His neat appearance, formal manners, and luxurious though not outlandish attire suggested wholesomeness but ultimately exuded...creepy.

"Heavens, not since I was about eight or nine," John began with an off-handed laugh. "Always been a city boy, no offence, not one for the woodsy stuff. My older brother Richard however used to slum about these woods on summer vay-cay, pretending he was a humble-bumble in order to shack up with local girls."

Did he say... "Richard? Slumming it?"

"Oh yes, terribly ungallant, I know," John drawled unashamedly as if he found the whole thing very funny, "but after Richie disappeared twenty years ago at first we all thought he'd simply moved on to swim in other waters, plough other fields, if you know what I mean. Of course, when he didn't come back, well you can imagine the scandal."

"I'm sorry..." Ella found herself saying while her brain wanted to bolt free and run screaming from the room. *Surely, he wasn't referring to her—to Cinderella's—Richard? Really a prince? Slumming it?*

It must be a coincidence, plenty of people were called Richard. Plenty of good-looking, unusually well-educated, woodcutters, who claimed to have no family and disappeared for weeks at a time...

"How do you like the arrows?" Prince John enquired of Sibylla. "Aren't they everything I promised?"

That talk of arrows jolted Ella from her own concerns. Could Prince John have supplied her sister with the magical black arrows? And at what cost? Surely Sibylla wouldn't knowingly mess with black magic?

Ella glanced down at Tomcat to see if he had likewise registered mention of the arrows, but Tomcat's little eyes were closed. Poor lad, she shouldn't have brought him. She had been selfish.

Ella didn't hear Sibylla's answer as a crystal bell chimed and suddenly they were all ambling down the hall, along the grand staircase and outside where they were directed to their seats on a small raised platform set up on one side of the market square which had been roped off to form a sporting arena for the archery contest.

Gracious. What a turnout.

Everyone and their granddad appeared to be squeezed in the square, those not holding aloft bows and arrows were waving small flags in the Charmington purple or clutching a food item, or toddler, or both. The crowd surged, cheering as the royal delegation found their seats. Sibylla and John's resembled thrones. Naturally.

Ella sighed. The humble-bumble seats awaited her as she shuffled forward, still holding onto Tomcat, out of habit. If ever there was a day to be stepped on, it was today. She was seated to the left of the Prince, who sat back, looking bored and fiddling with a large ring with a bulbous black stone.

Ug-*ly!*

Ella shrugged the uncharitable thought off and settled back. All things considered, she had a comfy seat and a good view. If she could convince someone to fetch her a cup of honey-bark tea, and a knee rug, this odd charade of Sibylla's could be endured in tolerable comfort.

Tomcat, however, appeared out of sorts, head drooping and uncharacteristically quiet. Was it the sudden realisation in a time when magic was forbidden, with everyone watching he carried his fate in his paws? Still, when had that stopped him before? She pretended to adjust his purple bow so that she could whisper, "Are you all right?"

Instead of answering, he curled into a tight ball on her lap. That spoke volumes. Poor Tom. Not that she could blame him. Crowds were overwhelming. The novelty of the splendour was wearing off, no doubt. Luxury swiftly became tiresome when it came with the catch of odious people and endless, pointless engagements. But they'd be back in the cottage in a few hours, comparing notes on who had the ugliest shoes just as she and her sisters would have done after a ball in the old days.

The old days... Perhaps if she got John talking about his brother Richard, she could confirm his Richard hadn't been *her* Richard, which clearly he definitely was not.

Plenty of people were called Richard, therefore plenty of people who also disappeared twenty years ago were just as likely to be named Richard. It made perfect logical sense.

Now, how to raise the topic?

Chapter 37

Archery contest – Part two

Ella turned to the prince. Small talk. She'd start with small talk.

"So... werewolf rats, what's that about?"

"Ugh, yes, tiresome little problem. All sorted now though, right, Wulf?" Prince John directed the last part of his statement to a man standing behind him. Though the man must have been there the whole time, somehow Ella hadn't seen him until now. A tall man with a wiry, nay—*graceful*—build, dressed entirely in black. A neatly trimmed beard was the only facial feature visible in the shadow of his hooded leather tunic.

Prince John said something else over his shoulder to Wulf who leaned forward to better hear his master. The movement exposed a chunky silver bracelet on one wrist. An odd item of jewellery for a man to wear, but stranger still, despite his leather clothing and the subtle outline of knives tucked in wrist braces, he moved in complete silence, graceful as a cobra.

"Coo-ee! Coo-ee!" A high-pitched duo of voices attracted Ella's attention. Out in the crowd the haberdashery twins, Millie and Sally, dressed in their finest and possibly competing for the title of who-could-wear-the-most-ruffles, shouted and waved lace handkerchiefs.

Ella waved back, which to her surprise raised a small cheer from the crowd. Goodness, everyone must be in high spirits if they were cheering for her, the black sheep!

She spotted Marge the midwife, wearing her short cape—red side out. Didn't that mean she was on duty?—standing beside the Cheltons. Arthur was pushing his way up to the golden velvet rope that separated the townspeople from their seated area. Arthur grinned, his thinning hair combed back, he looked quite dapper without his apron. "Long live the *true* queen!"

Ella ducked her head self-consciously as Sibylla nodded, the queen's red-painted lips twitched and bared back into an awkward impromptu smile, as if unsure whether the occasion called for a smile or a snarl due to lack of practice.

Ella was a little surprised to spot Axel, but then again, why wouldn't he be back at work after his adventures that morning? A fight, a fire and a break-up were probably just everyday occurrences for a henchman. He was out the front, where two archery targets had been set up, directing a dozen guardsmen who were awkwardly clutching pikes while trying to manoeuvre a large chain-bound strongbox on wheels.

Ah, this must be the fabled prize money.

Ella couldn't have been the only one thinking this as a collective and appreciative "Oooh!" rippled across the crowd.

The strongbox wasn't cooperating, possibly too heavy for the small wheels, it only wanted to turn left on the cobblestones despite Axel snapping at and bullying the men trying to steer the chest into position.

They should have practised last night, Ella found herself thinking. Although perhaps Axel had other things on his mind like chasing after other people's wives.

When Arthur was in charge of the guards, he wouldn't have made such an oversight. She sought out Arthur's face in the crowd again and was surprised to see him suddenly pale and turn away, disappearing into the townspeople.

Odd. Ella looked over her shoulder to see what Arthur had been looking at. It was Wulf. The man in black had a hand gripping the back of Prince John's chair. Across his knuckles was a jagged half-moon-shaped scar. Ella had seen a fresh wound of a similar pattern on Bron's hand a few weeks past. A wolf bite.

Well, that explained how he got the name...

Wulf turned toward her as if sensing she was staring. And though Ella couldn't see his eyes, shadowed as they were by the hood, when he turned in her direction Ella was certain the correct description of his eyes could only be *smouldering*.

She shivered and wanted to fan herself at the same time.

Magic preserve! Wulf was exactly the type of man she didn't want young Robinne running into! He was clearly smoking-hot trouble on a stick.

"Hear ye, hear ye!" Axel shouted, instantly causing the entire crowd to hush, apart from the continued squeak of wheels as the strongbox was wrestled into prime display beside the archery targets. Axel brushed a hand through his dark hair, a smouldering look of his own cast back at his men.

Ella leaned forward. There was no denying Axel was an attractive-looking man. Tall, confident, solid but not too solid, dark brooding eyes and... Ella shook herself. Regardless, he was not a nice person. As if being willed to prove her point, at that moment he backhanded a slap at one of the younger guards who dropped his pike when a wheel under the strongbox collapsed.

The crowd didn't laugh.

Not a snicker escaped their lips as three and a half thousand people's collective consciousness concluded *that box is heavy*. Very, *very*, heavy. And quickly calculated how much a thousand gold coins must weigh.

"About the same as a box of rocks," Ella muttered to herself and leaned back. Whether Sibylla had truly hauled a king's ransom out on display, or not, it didn't matter. Credit where credit was due. The moment was sheer drama.

"Hear ye, hear ye!" Axel resumed, his clear baritone ringing across the silent awestruck Charmington people. Even Prince John and his bodyguard-possibly-assassin, Wulf, appeared enthralled. "We are gathered here today to witness a grand archery contest. And awaiting the winner—"

"This box of rocks," Ella voiced internally when Axel revealed a key strung about his neck and pointed to the padlocked strongbox.

"Ooh!" breathed the crowd again, cueing a rakish smirk from Axel, as if he were somehow entirely responsible for the untold riches theoretically contained within and not just Sibylla's human keychain.

"Who here today is *skilled* enough," continued Axel, his voice rising to address the enraptured people, "is *noble* enough, true of heart and is outrightly *deserving enough* to claim such a treasure?"

Sibylla took that cue to suddenly stand up from her mock throne.

She unclasped something at her throat and her fur cloak fell to the ground in a pool of fabric. Revealing Sibylla in an extremely tight—perhaps even tighter than Ella had seen it yesterday—figure-hugging outfit of tailored tunic and men's pants in forest green.

There was a gasp from the crowd and a slight wail from someone fainting.

"Me likey," muttered Prince John under his breath. "Meow." He gave Sibylla a wink and added, "Go get 'em, tiger!"

Sibylla stepped down from the seating platform to walk through her people, who parted, bowing or kneeling as she passed, up to the archery butts. Axel bowed deeply before her as she turned to address the crowd, "My good and loyal people of Charmington, I stand before you, not as your true and rightful ruler, but as a girl, standing in front of a crowd, merely asking that you allow me a fair turn."

"Magic preserve," muttered Ella, crossing her arms, "what a farce!" Sibylla was practically daring people to prove their disloyalty by competing against her. That was really low. She glanced down at Tomcat for support, but he was still curled in a tight ball, shivering. Clearly, something was very wrong. Forget Sibylla and her foolish power plays, Ella had to get Tom back to the safety of her garden.

Ella rose to her feet as a murmuring spread across the crowd as people drew their own conclusions from the queen's address. Shakes of heads, doubtful glances at the bows they held, shrugs and mutterings. Sidelong glances cast at the alluring chest of gold.

Even the most dewy-eyed optimist seemed to be concluding that if they did engage in so-called *fair* competition there was a high risk of a case of sour grapes developing the following day, or night under cover of darkness when their neighbours were sitting at home and dwelling on who really deserved to have won that day...

Ella caught Sibylla and Axel exchanging glances. What were they waiting for? Axel gave a one-shouldered shrug and Ella recalled what Tom had said. This contest was an attempt to draw out Will Scarlett—or at least some rebel element. But Rum was dead, and Axel knew that. Did they suspect someone else? Who? Had Axel been sent to *spy* on the rebels, not join them?

She turned to Prince John, perched on the edge of his seat, and Wulf, who was not looking down at the crowd, but up. Scanning the rooftops and balconies above. He raised his scarred hand and Ella followed his motion just as someone in the crowd cried, "The Red Unicorn!"

Ella gasped as a mysterious red-cloaked and hooded figure appeared above on the queen's own balcony. Longbow drawn, deadly *black* arrow poised, aimed directly at Sibylla.

"Mummy!" yelped Prince John, ducking behind Ella's chair.

Wulf was off. One moment he was there, the next he was gone, a blur of motion, scaling the side of the castle.

Magic preserve!

The black arrow loosed.

—Zzing—clang!!!—

A resounding chime rang out as the arrowhead hit the padlock on the strongbox, shattering the lock in a jangle of chains falling free.

"Remember the Red Unicorn!" the mysterious figure shouted at the gawking queen and henchman, and then, with a swirl of red fabric, they pivoted to make their escape just as Wulf reached the top of the balcony and flung himself after the fleeing archer.

The surging crowd scattered, ramming into the platform and Ella stumbled, losing her balance. She grabbed for the back of the chair, one arm squeezing Tomcat close, and she found herself sheltering face to face with Prince John, before clambering back to her feet to see Wulf return to the balcony alone and empty-handed.

Chapter 38

Bait the Hook

"Ma'am, this way, this way!"

Ella looked up with a sigh of relief as Dirk Turpin appeared through the throng and assisted her across the courtyard to the royal carriage. Dirk opened the coach door and helped Ella inside. "There will be a delay leaving, I fear, ma'am," he said, casting apprehensive looks towards the castle gates. "The horses..."

Ella nodded. All the people trying to leave the square at once, it was only to be expected. "I don't mind waiting. Horses and frantic people don't mix."

Dirk touched his tricorn as if grateful she hadn't demanded they leave at once, and gently closed the door.

Ella placed Tomcat on a soft velvet cushion and wrapped the knee rug over him. Poor lad. He'd had an exhausting morning, not to mention all the smoke he had breathed in, it was no wonder he wasn't feeling well.

The horses' harness jingled, and the coach began to move at little more than a walking pace. Ella sat back and half-watched all the people on the road outside the castle, all milling about, like an ants' nest had been kicked over. No one was sure where to go.

Magic preserve, it was fair to say that today hadn't gone as planned.

That reminded her, she must read those instructions. What exactly did Sibylla need to negotiate with the regent of the neighbouring kingdom that she'd go so low as to actually ask—or *demand*, as the case may be—her disgraced sister's help?

She felt for the instructions in her pocket. Still there. Good. She'd read them tonight once Tom was safely home, she really didn't want to add another drama into the mix right this moment. Goodness, could it really be possible that Prince John's brother was the same Richard who married Cinderella? Was John trying to lay some claim to the Charming throne? That might explain Sibylla's need to call Ella in for help.

Richard and Cinderella's wedding ceremony had been humble and modest, a country affair as befitting a woodcutter. Everyone in Wyld kingdom knew that when members of the Charming family married, they gave up their claim to wealth, magic and all its trappings. It was the price. It was the system they had followed for years—centuries. The only way to ensure that their peaceful way of life maintained its balance. Certainly many Charmings had married into wealthy families or had become the founders of some of the well-to-do families of Charmington, but always, always, they gave up their magic.

What exactly could the repercussions be if Cinderella had unwittingly married a prince, not a woodcutter? But no, that would make Richard a liar. Wouldn't it?

Ella tried to push the nagging thought away only to have it replaced with another as the townspeople, cloaked mostly in traditional forest colours of brown and green, streamed past the carriage window.

Who was the red-cloaked person on the balcony?

Ella tried to recall the faces in the contest crowd. Ruling out those that simply couldn't be in two places at once.

Who was missing from that picture? Bron, Ginny, Robinne... Again, the three that had occupied her mind the last couple of days. Was that a coincidence? Surely not. And what of the arrow they had shot? It was black, but that proved nothing. Robinne could have made that shot. Shooting a padlock wasn't magical. It was a testament to skill. Who else did she know that could have achieved such a feat? Who else wasn't down in the crowds?

Arthur.

He had disappeared a few moments before. The look on Arthur's face appeared in her mind. His expression of horror. What had he seen that had upset him so? Was it Wulf? Or something else? And would Arthur have had enough time to get up to the balcony? Once, long ago Arthur had been the Captain of the guards and had served as Ella's own bodyguard, but he was not a young man any more. Arthur could not have outrun Wulf.

And what did any of this have to do with poor Tom April?

Instead of having received Rum's confession about attempting to kill young Tom, Rum himself was dead and yet someone was still running around shooting black arrows and trading on the story of the Red Unicorn.

The coach came to a halt and Ella leaned over to have a look at what had caused traffic to stop when her eye was caught by a passer-by wearing a short red cape. An idea occurred. She had been going about this all wrong—and Sibylla of all people had shown her the way.

If you wanted to catch something, sometimes hunting wasn't the answer. It was time to try bait.

Ella opened the window catch and slid the sash down. "Marge!"

The red-cloaked person stopped walking and turned. Marge the midwife. Her eyes lit up on seeing Ella waving to her from one of the royal carriages. "Lady Ella, how lovely to see you again," Marge trilled, peering up, "I love your outfit."

Ella dispensed with the niceties. "You recall that handsome new henchman, Tom April?"

Marge nodded eagerly, her eyes practically doubled in size like a belly on a fat frog after consuming a big meal, as if sensing she was ground-zero in the gossip-spreading chain.

"Well, you'll never guess, but I found him gravely injured and passed out in the snow, mere feet from my cottage, clearly he had been set upon!"

Marge clamped her little hands to her cherub cheeks. "Oh my goodness! Whoever would do such a dreadful thing?"

"I don't currently know. The poor lad has been unconscious these past two days. But fortunately, due to my tender care and medicines, I'm sure he'll wake about teatime and no doubt his attacker's identity will be the first thing on his lips."

Marge licked her own lips as if imagining hearing those words.

"I must go, I only popped into town to fetch more bandages and of course inform Sibylla that I have her henchman safely tucked up in my cottage." She nodded good day and slid the window up, leaving Marge looking slightly giddy or gossip drunk in the main thoroughfare as the carriage rolled away.

The morning hadn't gone as planned. Would the night?

CHAPTER 39

GROWTH SPURT

RIVERSIDE COTTAGE, WYLD ENCHANTMENT WOODS.

Ella's head was drooping as the coach bumped and swayed along the old road when on the cushion beside her, Tomcat stirred.

"What can I get you? Water? Medicine?" Ella asked as he opened his eyes.

Tomcat shook his whole body and stretched, claws extended into the velvet cushions, for all the world looking like a regular cat waking from a long nap.

"Tilly...?" Ella breathed, wondering for a second if this was still Tom.

"I'm feeling much better," Tom answered, "it was just..."

Ella let out a breath she didn't know she'd held and nodded sympathetically. "You don't have to explain, the crowds, everyone watching, judging, I understand."

Tomcat grimaced. "Partly but, I don't know...I was fine until we went into the library, then I felt overcome, hopeless, like...I don't know. And there was a terrible smell."

"Well, thank you very much," Ella said bitingly. "You live year-round in winter with only snow-melt for water and see how many baths you take!"

"No, no, it's not you," Tomcat soothed. "You smell lovely, like your cottage, you smell of home-baked apple pie."

"Apple pie?" Ella muttered disbelievingly and covertly sniffed the neckline of her purple coat dress.

"No, weirdly it reminded me of the black arrow, remember I told you it smelled unpleasant? Only in the library, the smell was much, much stronger. It was awful. It smelled like...death."

"Hmm," Ella tutted thoughtfully and raised the back of her hand, which Prince John had slobbered on, under Tomcat's nose.

He flinched and gagged. "That's it! That's the smell. Do you know what it is?"

"That is the taint of black magic," Ella said. This answered one question. The prince must have been the source of the black arrows. No wonder Sibylla was upset enough to enlist her help, Prince John *was* dabbling with black magic. "I can't sense anything. Without my own magic bound, I'm blind to it."

"But I don't have any magic, how can it affect me?"

"You're a talking cat, I think you might have a little magic." Ella looked up realising the carriage had stopped moving.

A moment later Dirk's smiling face was at the door, offering his arm and assisting her down from the coach. Her boots crunched in fresh powdery snow. Tomcat's earlier prediction had been correct, while they had been in Charmington a layer of snow had coated her part of Wyld Enchantment Woods. Dirk's breath fanned out in clouds of steam as he escorted Ella to the edge of the river. He squinted across at the pumpkins, the large green leaves were dusted with snow, the sloping roof and dormer windows of her cottage likewise nestled under a picturesque white blanket. Dirk patted her hand, doffed his tricorn and bid her good day.

As soon as his footsteps faded the pumpkin stirred. Curious strands perked up. Ella set Tom down so that he could cross the frozen river by himself and took a moment to enjoy the welcome sight of her home. She recalled the day many years ago when they'd finished building and she had stood on this same spot with Richard, who had said, 'I couldn't have built her without you, charming Ella, I think you should have the honour of naming our humble abode. What shall it be?'

"Riverside cottage," Ella murmured, lost in her memories. Of course, it had been summer then. Everything was lush and glossy, the apple trees in the orchard, the river swirling by their feet, bubbling like laughter and the whole world had been filled with promise.

"Um, Ella," Tomcat said, having leapt onto the first river steppingstone, now embedded in ice, and flicking his tail. His little head tilted left and right. "How many dormer windows did the cottage have this morning?"

"Two...of course..." Ella broke from her daydream to stare up at the little lead glass attic windows nestled in the sloping roof. Her eyes must be playing tricks. There were three windows now.

"Magic preserve!" Ella clapped her hands to her cheeks as the midwife had done. She set off across the sheet of ice, Tomcat trotting along beside her. "I can't believe it!" Ella said, mostly to herself, "it hasn't grown in twenty years!"

"Grown?" Tomcat said, whiskers fanning.

"The cottage was built with wyld magic pumpkin seeds," Ella explained, "I sort of trained it to do what we wanted." Suddenly all the creaking and groaning last night made a lot more sense. It wasn't the wind in the trees, the house itself was waking from dormancy, it had begun growing again.

"Wow! That's amazing, so the whole cottage is like the *Cinderella* story—but instead of a coach, you turned a pumpkin into a house!" Tomcat jumped up onto the lawn where the giant strands of pumpkin vines reached out to pat him. "Hey! I think it missed me!"

"I expect it is grateful for all the extra protein," Ella joked as she and Tomcat climbed the porch steps and entered the front door. After removing her boots, Ella paused at the foot of the stairs to tug her slippers on. She wasn't stalling, of course not. There was nothing to fear.

"What do you suppose is up there?" Tomcat peered up the stairs.

Ella shrugged. "Another room, I suppose. Once I trained the magic to create the cottage it just seemed to understand what Richard needed. One time he told me a cider press grew overnight when it was time to harvest the apples, but nothing has changed since he disappeared."

Tomcat's little pink mouth popped open. "Richard disappeared? You didn't tell me that? What happened?"

"Oh, didn't I...?" Ella murmured distractedly, the suspicions seeded in her mind from the conversation with Prince John reappeared, but she pushed them aside. It couldn't be true. Richard wasn't a liar, he was honourable, hard-working and loyal. He was a woodcutter. Not a prince slumming it to shack up with local girls! Besides, Richard had been a husband and father.

Ella gripped the handrail and climbed the stairs. "It wasn't long after Cinderella passed away, Richard was heartbroken, we hoped that their child would give him purpose, but alas he just withdrew into himself." Ella swallowed and wiped her cuff across her eyes. "Lawks, I really need to dust better."

"Oh Ella, that's just so sad! And he abandoned his own child?" Tom waited at the top of the stairs for her to catch up, peering down the hall to a simple wooden door that matched the others, for all the world looking like it had always been there.

Ella shook her head. "Richard took the child with him. They were here one day, and the next, gone..." Ella recalled standing in this hallway all those years ago. Calling Richard's name. Her voice echoing through the empty cottage. He had left without saying goodbye. How she had cried that day.

"It won't be dangerous, will it?" Tomcat whispered as she reached for the new door handle on the mysterious new door.

"Tosh!" Ella muttered, sucking in a breath, she turned the knob and pushed the door open.

"Tosh?" replied Tomcat, sounding amused, "I haven't heard you use..." His voice trailed off as they entered the new little room, and he stood up on his hind legs in wonder and joined Ella in clapping hands to cheeks as they gawked at a strange contraption that filled the room.

An odd wooden item built of many levels and platforms, several little cupboards branched out to connect via ropes and ladders and columns bound with thick twine.

"It's like a treehouse..." Ella began when Tomcat suddenly sprung up into one of the cupboards and popped out a moment later at the top of the contraption where a willow basket was perched. "...for a cat," Ella concluded.

"It's the best thing *ever!*" Tomcat purred, darting here and there, running along the little walkways, clawing at the roped columns, pouncing from one padded bed to another. "Is this for me, do you think?"

For the second time that day, Ella smiled.

"It would appear so." She glanced out to the garden. The swaying pumpkin strands made a bow-like motion and then folded gently around the giant pumpkin, like seeking rest after the growth spurt spent on creating this surprise for the cottage's newest member.

"I'll put the kettle on." Ella hummed to herself as she ventured back downstairs. What exactly did this mean in terms of Tom's human body and its pumpkin stasis? Perhaps the pumpkin egg was going to take some time in hatching? One week, two? Surely Tom wouldn't be stuck as a cat for longer than a month, right?

CHAPTER 40

SOMETHING WICKED THIS WAY COMES

ELLA'S STOMACH WAS RUMBLING WHEN SHE WALKED INTO HER KITCHEN. Despite planning on filling her pockets with canapés from the castle at the archery contest she'd managed no such thing, and now she thought about it, she hadn't had a bite to eat before dashing out to the Crossroads tavern that morning.

Ella went into her pantry and surveyed the shelves. Her stock of preserves was running very low. Half a dozen jams and chutneys. Nevertheless, she must take some to Robinne, the lass would need it more than her. Only Ella's pride stood between her and hunger, as despite their differences Sibylla wouldn't let her starve. She fetched an apple chutney from the shelf. Goodness, did Rum even own the tavern, or was it rented? Ella felt a guilty start that she couldn't answer this simple question. Poor Robinne, what would become of the lass now? Would she go to Nottingham with her aunt when Ginny took up her position in Nottingham Palace? That seemed the most likely thing. Ugh. Right under the nose of that creepy little prince.

Ella lifted the kettle off the wood stove and then slowly put it back down again. Had the cooker changed? Yes...it didn't have a built-in water boiler before. Gracious, what a genius idea. Just think that would save so much time and effort boiling kettles for bath day!

"Tom, are you hungry?" Ella called over her shoulder, after placing a couple of eggs in a pot of water and adding a slice of ginger to the kettle as she'd seen Tom do. "I'm putting the eggs on. You want soft-boiled or hard?"

Then she sat at the kitchen table and took out the golden envelope from her pocket. In Sibylla's familiar cursive the words *Important Task. June.* was written on the outer.

June? Was it June?

Ella reached for the copy of the *Nottingham Times* still on the table. Why yes, so it was. Living in an eternal state of winter the months seemed to all merge into one. If it wasn't for the apples in the orchard continuing their cycle through the seasons, she could well believe it was December all year round.

Ella found herself staring at the envelope. *Important task. June.*

Had she seen this written somewhere before?

Tom's instructions!

Ella fetched the instructions they had taken from Tom's room the day before and set them side by side with the envelope.

Instructions for April.

Now that she compared the two, it struck her how squashed up the word 'for' was. And perhaps she was imagining it, but was it written in a slightly darker shade of ink? As if fresher?

Ella placed her finger over the line, obscuring the darker word.

Instructions. April.

Of course, the instructions weren't *for* Tom April, they had been *written* in April! Magic preserve, someone had altered these instructions.

Someone had made it *seem* the queen wanted Tom to carry the mirror.

Ginny knew where Tom's room at the castle was... Could she be working in conjunction with or without Rum and Robinne to fuel or finance some rebellion in revenge for what happened to her sister Yara?

Revenge for the fate of her sister... It seemed such an obvious motivation.

Tomcat's footsteps padded down the stairs and he popped into the kitchen. "Someone's coming," he said.

"So soon?" Ella stood up, shunting her chair back. "I distinctly said teatime!"

"What are you talking about?"

"I was going to tell you." And Ella hurriedly explained the rumour she had deliberately told Marge, knowing the midwife would spread it.

"Why would you do that?" Tomcat cried, horrified, as Ella hobbled to the front door.

There was a knock.

"Don't open it! It's the killer!" Tom flung himself in front of Ella and pressed his paws against the door, barring her way.

Ella rolled her eyes at his dramatics, and called out through the safety of the stout door, in her best rendition of a helpless, elderly woman, "Who's there, dearie?"

"Cheapcuts."

"Cheapcuts! The butcher's boy!" Tomcat's mouth was wider than a frog swallowing a banana. "I did not see that coming!"

"Don't be foolish," Ella muttered, scooting him aside with her slippered foot so that she could open the door. "He's delivering the bacon you wanted yesterday."

"Oh, right!" Tomcat's little shoulders slumped as he pooled in a relieved puddle of fur on the floorboards.

"Good afternoon, mistress Lady Ella," Cheapcuts gulped, his Adam's apple bobbing. The gangly youth pulled his cap off and clutched it in both hands as if he'd just remembered some instructions on manners that his mother Martha had drilled into him. "Got yer bacon." He hooked a thumb over at a laden handcart across the stream.

"Thank you, Cheapcuts," Ella said, "can you take it around to the backdoor? You'll see I have a meat safe just beyond. And you can call me good mother Ella, if you like."

"Yes, mistress lady good mother Ella," Cheapcuts responded, bobbing his head and quickly dashing across the river to fetch the side of bacon, taking a moment to enjoy a slide across the ice, he was back in a flash and disappeared around the side of the house.

Something made Ella glance over to where Cheapcuts' empty cart waited for his return when movement and colour caught her eye. Red against white.

A red-cloaked person was approaching through the snow-covered forest.

Chapter 41

Remember the unicorn

With a steady hand, Ella closed the front door. "Tom, would you mind supervising Cheapcuts out the back? And see if he would like to pick fresh apples for his parents. You will find pails in Tinkerbelle's barn."

"Your orchard still grows apples? That I have to see..." Tomcat darted down the hallway and into the kitchen. "Hey—the backdoor has a cat flap now!"

Ella only nodded, it seemed the house had thought of everything to accommodate Tom. That was good, should anything happen to her, he would be taken care of. She took a couple of deep breaths and picked up her walking stick, before opening the front door.

"I am not a helpless old lady, I am not a helpless old lady," she muttered under her breath as she trekked down the porch steps, across the lawn and stood on the edge of the riverbank, her slippers squelched in the wet.

Oops, she hadn't put her boots back on, too late now. Ella did her best to stand up straight, and ignore the freezing damp seeping into her toes, while she waited as the person in red approached through the pine trees. Their walk had a slight sway, and beneath the cloak, a shapely figure, whoever it was, they were female. And looped across her shoulder a longbow.

Ella recalled Baker Bron had alleged the person in red who had been searching Tom's body was a man. It must have been a lie. To protect his wife Ginny. Who else could it be? After all, Ginny bought the tickets for the stagecoach. It all added up.

"I would stop there, if I were you," Ella called as the cloaked woman reached the edge of the river, "the ice is thinner than it looks."

The woman halted. She pushed back her hood, to reveal dark curls and a familiar heart-shaped face.

"Robinne..." Magic preserve, Ella's heart sank. Of course, the lass was an excellent archer, with or without a magic arrow she could have easily shot Tom.

Robinne eyed the ice. "Very well, I'll say what I came to say here."

Ella swallowed. Nearby, she could sense the pumpkin stirring, whispering to itself as if debating its next move, likewise, its attention fixed on the girl.

"Rum had a conversation with me last night, told me some things that have been kept from me. Things he said you knew, like who my father was."

Ella nodded. "Go on."

Robinne shrugged as if the details were not important. "One thing he said, trust Ella Charming."

Ella felt a hot sting in her eyes, but she resisted the urge to wipe them.

"So, I came to apologise for my past behaviour, and to let you know Rum's funeral will be a week tomorrow, once we've had time to get word to his family up in the deep mountains. I hope you will come."

Ella nodded. "I'm truly sorry for your loss."

Robinne nodded, and as if she'd done what she came for, turned to go.

Ella's unspoken fears faded away. Elation swelled her heart. She called out, "That was a fine shot today. Your father would've been proud."

Robinne just lifted her hand, neither denying nor claiming the feat with the strongbox lock, but Ella saw the corner of the girl's lips curl up as she turned away back into the forest.

"Long live the revolution," Ella whispered under her breath, turning back across the lawn, her water-sodden sheepskin slippers dampening her relieved mood somewhat.

Goodness, was there more grass poking out than yesterday? Everything was growing. Where had Tomcat and Cheapcuts got to? How long did it take to fill a bucket of apples?

Ella hobbled around the house to the backyard when she heard Cheapcuts calling her name and a muffled thumping from the stable. The door on Tinkerbelle's barn had been barred, how did that happen...?

Fresh footprints in the snow crisscrossed the back garden and the cottage backdoor hung open. Footsteps echoed inside the cottage; someone was stomping *down* the stairs.

Oh dear...

Ella stepped back as from inside a man said, "He's not in the barn, he's not upstairs, where oh where, is young Tom April?" And Axel stalked out onto the porch.

Ella swallowed, and clutched her dress-coat to her throat, "Wh-what do you want with Tom April?"

Axel grinned and parted his hands. "I'm just concerned, my newest recruit is missing…" He trailed a finger along the porch railing. "He didn't make the midnight coach."

The midnight coach.

Ella swallowed. "You bought the tickets, not Ginny."

"Now why would you say that?" Axel's smile was brittle. "Everyone knows Tom has run off with the baker's wife."

"Or some people would like other people to think that," Ella found herself saying. "Was that actually your plan? Run off with Ginny?"

Axel's expression wavered; his brow pinched with regret.

Ella was struck dumb. Regret was an expression she knew intimately because she'd seen herself wearing it in the looking glass each morning. He actually *cared* for Ginny.

"What went wrong? She found out what you're really like? She broke it off, didn't she? But then she made you think she wanted you back, when the truth was, she just wanted the arrow to help save her family from financial ruin. And that…and that made you think about how to boost your own finances by stealing the mirror and blaming newcomer Tom for the theft!"

Axel laughed, cutting her off. "Now, now, good mother Ella, or Lady Ella, or whatever you want to be called. You're a smart old lady, so I'll be direct." Axel's smile deepened, but his eyes were cold. "You know I can't hurt you, on account of our fine, and noble queen, but *you will* tell me where you have hidden Tom April."

He slapped a palm to the wall of the cottage. "This is a really nice home, it's no castle, but it sure is fine. Sturdy. Safe. Secure. But you know why I like living in a *stone* castle and not a wooden cottage?" He winked. "Stone doesn't burn down in the middle of the night."

CHAPTER 42

THE TRAP IS SPRUNG

"ENOUGH STALLING, WHERE ARE YOU HIDING TOM APRIL?"

"I am not hiding him," Ella began, gesturing to the far side of her house as Axel's face hardened, and he took a menacing step towards her. "He's in the pumpkin patch."

"Nice of you to cooperate." Axel's expression lightened and he turned and strode off around the porch with Ella following.

If Axel was surprised by the giant sprawling pumpkin vines, dusted in snow, he hid it well, muttering something about a bizarre frozen jungle was as good a place to hide as any.

"Did you steal Robinne's cloak that night? Were you trying to get her blamed as well?" Ella questioned.

"Long live the revolution," Axel said, striding to the edge of the patch.

"Huh! You may have loved Ginny, but you don't care about the people. You just thought the mirror was something to sell, something that wouldn't be missed because it was broken. Right?"

Axel bent a few vines back and entered the overgrown garden without answering.

"What I don't understand is why you shot Tom. You could have just as easily pretended the queen was sending you both to Nottingham."

Axel tapped the side of his nose. "That would have left a trail."

"Of course, that's why you killed Rum. Once the mirror theft was discovered, Rum could link you to it. First, you threatened him, broke his arm to keep him silent, but it wasn't enough. You had to remove him from the chain."

Axel waved her away. "Quit talking, go back inside, you don't have to see this…"

Ella stood her ground. "I've been trying to tell you, there's nothing to see, Tom didn't survive the arrow." She gestured to the wall of vines. "I buried him myself, it's why the plant is thriving."

Axel paused; eyes narrowed as if weighing up the truth. "I guess that means *you* are the last link…"

"You can't hurt me! You said so yourself!"

Axel shrugged. Gestured to the living wall of green that enclosed them. "But who's to see? Who would even look for you here?"

Around them, the pumpkins stirred. The eerie whispering picked up and Axel smiled. "I nearly bought it, but I can *hear* you, Tom. You come out now and I won't harm this nosey old woman."

The rustling increased. A vine swayed as if something moved through the undergrowth and Axel turned towards it, calling out, "Just toss me the mirror and no one gets hurt. We go our separate ways."

"I'm afraid you're too late, I gave Sibylla back the mirror," Ella gloated at his back. "Didn't you know?"

"What!" Axel spun around. His face was a mask of anger. "You did what, you stupid, old woman!"

Ella's triumph faltered. She started to back up. Heart pounding. Oh dear. Sibylla might have a point about her pride...

"Don't you walk away from me!" Axel shouted, jabbing a finger at Ella, while down at his feet tendrils of vine twined about his boots.

Axel lunged for her, but the snaking vines tripped him. He kicked at the vines as another curled about his elbow and he was trapped.

Ella leaned over him. "Well, well, it turns out you were right after all, I don't need to see this, and just as you said, *no one* will think to look for you *here*."

A flash of panic stripped off his anger as Ella turned away. "Come back here!" Axel shouted, then yelped, the sound of him thrashing grew fainter as she hobbled back to the stables.

"Cheapcuts, are you all right?" Ella called, lifting the bar that had been placed over the barn door.

The butcher's boy blinked in the daylight. "Mr Axel locked me in. Did you know your cat can talk?"

Tomcat raced out from the stables and rushed around the side of the house.

Ella tried to look innocent. "Can he? Lawks. Talk you say? Are you sure it wasn't a trick of the light?"

But Tomcat was already shouting and calling her to come to the front yard, ruining her attempt to keep his secret.

"Maybe it's something he only does in times of great danger?" Ella began but then gave up on the pointless subterfuge as she and Cheapcuts ventured to the front lawn where Axel was trussed up in a cocoon of vines, wriggling and swearing like a very angry caterpillar.

"You've got nothing on me!" Axel shouted.

"Except you knew Tom had the mirror, no one else knew that so you must have been the one to get him to unwittingly carry it. I think the queen will believe my word over yours when I explain things, especially since I returned her mirror."

"Do you think you get out of this squeaky clean?" Axel snarled. "I'm not the one who owns a talking cat! Magic is banned on pain of death!"

"A talking cat, what a load of nonsense, who would believe that?" Ella tutted. "Have you heard of anything sillier, Cheapcuts?"

Cheapcuts looked a little confused but then shook his head. "Talking cats don't exist!"

"Cut me free, boy," Axel shouted at Cheapcuts. "Cut me free, or I will gut you like a fish!"

"You will do no such thing!" Tomcat said, standing over the vine-tangled henchman. "You're a disgrace to guardsmen! Bullying and threatening. I am ashamed of you."

Ella stood back as Tomcat directed the pumpkin to hoist the bound henchman up over the ice and onto the waiting handcart like a sack of cussing potatoes.

"Maybe you should wait here," Tomcat said to Ella when she went to put on her boots and fetch her walking stick, "it's a long walk back to the castle."

"I appreciate your compassion for my knees, but you'll need my testimony if you want this awful excuse for a human to be held accountable. As much as I want to believe Sibylla will embrace the word of a talking cat who claims to work for her, I'm also inclined to think she might just as likely lock you up."

"Oh," was all Tomcat said, and he was unnaturally quiet while he and Cheapcuts hooked Tinkerbelle up to the cart to help with pulling the additional load.

Axel however was not prepared to go quietly. "This isn't over!" He shouted at Ella. "You can't hide behind the queen forever. Maybe you win today, but you made a bad mistake crossing me! You too, cat!"

Cheapcuts leaned over and whispered something in Axel's ear. And to Ella's surprise, the henchman suddenly fell silent. He paled.

The butcher's boy clicked his tongue and taking Tinkerbelle's reins, he guided the delivery cart onward.

"What did you say to Axel?" Ella enquired of the butcher's boy when they were all walking in silence under the snowy trees.

"Weren't nothing. Just said me gutting knives are already in this here cart." Cheapcuts shrugged and touched his cap, apologetically. "You never know when you might come across a fresh kill in the forest, and as me pa taught me, meat is meat."

Ella blinked. There was a thought to turn her vegetarian. *Meat is meat.*

Chapter 43

Resolution?

Chelton butchery, Southgate square, Charmington.

On approaching the southern gates into Charmington, Cheapcuts, by virtue of having the youngest and quickest legs, was sent to run on ahead while Ella and Tomcat lead Tinkerbelle and their cussing cargo into the small courtyard at the back of the Chelton butchery in Southgate square.

From there word was sent on to the castle and shortly after the queen's coach was seen entering the quietest part of town, made less quiet by Axel's shouting and protests.

Dirk opened the coach door and assisted Sibylla from the carriage. She curled back her lips and cast distasteful looks at the common surroundings, as if disinclined to even let her high-heeled boots touch the cobblestones. Martha and Chelton bobbed and curtseyed every time the queen glanced in their direction.

"I don't appreciate having my time wasted or the captain of my guards bound up like a Christmas ham, so you better have an excellent reason," Sibylla told Ella.

"Axel has been stealing from you, he was going to run off with your magic mirror and blame the theft on the new henchman, Tom April—who he then tried to kill—and he murdered Rum the craftsman to cover up his trail of past thefts."

"It's all lies!" Axel snarled, wriggling against the pumpkin vine coils.

"Can you prove any of this?" Sibylla arched a perfectly sculptured eyebrow.

"Ahhh..." Proof. What proof did Ella have? She'd given Sibylla back a mirror her sister didn't even know was missing, Tom's injured human body was out of sight encased in a giant pumpkin, and no one had seen how Rum died.

Ella held her head up high. "I give you my word."

Sibylla's dark eyes narrowed. "Very well, while Axel has always been diligent in fulfilling his duties, I—"

"She's got a talking cat!" Axel spat. "A magical talking cat!"

All eyes turned to Tomcat, who said, "Meow."

Sibylla rolled her eyes and pointed at Axel. "You. Sixty days in the lockup. If you cross me again I will execute you myself."

"Won't happen again, thank you, your majesty."

"Shut up."

"Yes, Majesty."

Ella was incensed. "Is that all? Sixty days and then he's free? But he killed Rum!"

"Enough!" Sibylla snapped and held up her hand to quell any other protests from Ella or Axel. "I have made my decision. I have quite enough to deal with running this kingdom without my staff bickering—"

"Staff?" Ella baulked. "Who me? I don't *work* for you!"

"You have no idea what our kingdom is facing, do you?" Sibylla tapped a toe and crossed her arms. "Did you read those instructions or not?"

"Yes...?" Ella found she couldn't meet her sister's eye. "Tonight, definitely."

Sibylla threw her hands up in exasperation. "See that you do!" She stalked off, instructing Dirk to have someone come fetch Axel while the coachman assisted her back into the carriage as the Chelton family bobbed up and down like a Mexican wave of three.

"Your ladyship, won't you join us for some supper?" Martha invited Ella into their home once the carriage had rolled off. "We're having lasagne, one of Arthur's vegetarian recipes."

"Ooh, my favourite!" said Tomcat.

"I heard that," muttered Axel from the handcart.

"No one else did, you big useless pudding," Martha said tartly, and she nodded to her husband, "Chelton, my love, why don't you save the queen the bother of collecting this troublesome *ham*?"

Axel whimpered as the butcher loomed large above him and even Ella held her breath.

Meat is meat...

But whatever they both assumed was about to unfold, Chelton merely grabbed a handful of the vines coiled about Axel and hefted him up into one shoulder with no apparent strain, and after giving his wife and Ella a cheery wave he followed after the queen's coach, with Cheapcuts skipping along at his father's side.

"Once saw him carry a bear three miles," Martha confided to Ella with no small amount of pride in her voice. Then the butcher's wife gestured to the backdoor. "Right this way your ladyship, and you too, Mr Cat in cravat."

Ella smiled her thanks to Martha and then looked down at Tomcat. "Cat in cravat. Hmm. I like that."

Tomcat shrugged. "It has a certain ring to it. It's no 'Puss in boots' though..."

"Who?"

CHAPTER 44

HOME AGAIN, HOME AGAIN

The cluckoo clock ticked pleasantly on the mantelpiece above the hearth in Ella's parlour. The string of fairy lights glowed merrily, bathing the snug room in a golden hue.

The hour was late, but Ella felt restless, dwelling on the events of the past few days. She leaned forward on her rocking chair to pick up the copy of the *Nottingham Times*. Perhaps finishing the crossword would distract her agitated brain.

Tomcat trotted into the parlour. He circled three times before settling into the pile of velvet coach cushions beside the glowing hearth. "Nice of the queen to give you these cushions."

"Uh-huh," Ella agreed. "Lawks, very kind."

"And it's very kind of you to let me stay here while I recover. Thank you."

Ella cleared her throat. "Think nothing of it. That's what friends do. Say no more."

"Is everything okay? You seem a little out of sorts."

Ella flicked the newspaper pages back and forth in annoyance. "I failed to get justice for you or Rum."

"Nonsense. You found out what happened, you weren't silent and you stood up for what was right. You made a difference and I'm grateful. Once I've fully recovered and am a guardsman again, I will hold Axel accountable. With your help, of course." He curled into a tight ball. "We made a good team."

"Let's not get soppy. This is just a temporary arrangement. I don't see us having any more quirky adventures, running around and solving crime in Wyld Woods."

"I guess not. It was fun though. It made me think it wouldn't be so bad if I was stuck as a cat for a while," Tomcat said sleepily, his little pink nose sticking out from his fur. "You made a great sidekick."

"What? *You're* the sidekick—clearly—I'm the one putting all the clues together."

"If you say so." He yawned, his white fur golden in the low light. "What shall we do while we wait for the next mystery to solve?"

"If you wanted to do pinecone-based arts and crafts, I'm afraid I threw the last pinecone on the fire about five minutes ago—"

Owwwooowoooh!

A howl cut the night air and echoed about the forest. Tomcat's ears flicked upright, and his hackles raised. "Did you hear that?"

From her rocking chair, Ella said, "Just a wolf, nothing to fear. We're quite safe on our little island."

"Surrounded by ice, not water! The wolf can walk right across!" Tomcat rose from the pile of soft cushions. "I better go outside and sleep in the coop. To protect the chickens, like we agreed."

"That's very diligent of you but unnecessary. Wolves' claws and ice are not a good mix. I've seen it. Poor things, they slide all over and can't stand up—like a baby deer just born. They've learned to keep away."

Tomcat's tail flicked. "But what about the newspaper articles? What if it's not a regular wolf? What if it's a *wolf-man*?"

Ella glanced at the *Nottingham Times* on her lap. Every other article and advert was werewolf centric: wolfsbane sales, wolf-proofing services, ten ways to tell if your teen was a werewolf. The whole of Nottingham seemed to be in a grip of werewolf fever.

Thank goodness the Charmington populous were more sensible. "Nonsense. A bunch of foolish people jumping at their own shadows."

Owwwooowoooh!

The howl was closer.

Oh dear...

Ella shuddered, imagining a slavering half-man, half-beast, prowling beneath the pines, creeping closer and closer.

"Ella, did you lock the front door?"

~The End~

Book Two in the Series:

What's the Time of Death, Mr Wolf?

Out Soon!

Acknowledgements

Special Thanks to the Dunedin Chapter of the RWNZ. Without the unwavering support of the members during the period 2020 to 2022, this book may have never come about.

Thank you to **Karen Johnson** for the proofreading.

A very big **Thank You** to my lovely beta readers, in particular **Kay Mercer** and **Angela Oliver**, your feedback was invaluable.

About the Author

Kura Carpenter is a New Zealand author and was the 2019 recipient of the Sir Julius Vogel award for Best New Talent.
When not writing, Kura enjoys convincing strangers that greyhounds make the best pets.

Web: **www.kuracarpenter.com**
Instagram: @kura.carpenter